MW00772632

MURDER AT THE MATTERHORN

T. A. WILLIAMS

Boldwood

First published in Great Britain in 2023 by Boldwood Books Ltd.

Copyright © T. A. Williams, 2023

Cover Design by Nick Castle

Cover Photography: Shutterstock

The moral right of T. A. Williams to be identified as the author of this work has been asserted in accordance with the Copyright, Designs and Patents Act 1988.

All rights reserved. No part of this book may be reproduced in any form or by any electronic or mechanical means, including information storage and retrieval systems, without written permission from the author, except for the use of brief quotations in a book review.

This book is a work of fiction and, except in the case of historical fact, any resemblance to actual persons, living or dead, is purely coincidental.

Every effort has been made to obtain the necessary permissions with reference to copyright material, both illustrative and quoted. We apologise for any omissions in this respect and will be pleased to make the appropriate acknowledgements in any future edition.

A CIP catalogue record for this book is available from the British Library.

Paperback ISBN 978-1-80483-268-4

Large Print ISBN 978-1-80483-267-7

Hardback ISBN 978-1-80483-269-1

Ebook ISBN 978-1-80483-265-3

Kindle ISBN 978-1-80483-266-0

Audio CD ISBN 978-1-80483-274-5

MP3 CD ISBN 978-1-80483-273-8

Digital audio download ISBN 978-1-80483-272-1

Boldwood Books Ltd
23 Bowerdean Street
London SW6 3TN
www.boldwoodbooks.com

To Mariangela and Christina with love as always

1

TUESDAY EVENING

Anna's Aunt Domenica, known to everybody in the family as Zia Menca, was unlike any other ninety-year-old I had ever met. When Anna and her sister had asked her what she wanted as a birthday present, the reply had been a new external hard drive for her computer. I have only one aunt of a similar vintage and I know for a fact that she wouldn't have known what a hard drive was and, even if she had known, she would have dismissed it along with anything to do with computers as the work of the Devil. Zia Menca was a very different kettle of fish. Not only did she own a computer and know far more about technology and the Internet than I did, but she also had her own blog with a following of tens of thousands on social media and she produced regular podcasts.

Yes, she was quite some lady.

I glanced at my watch and saw that it was almost ten o'clock. Virgilio and Lina had been looking after Oscar all evening while Anna and I came to the grand old lady's birthday party along with most of the inhabitants of the little village outside Florence where she lived. I knew we would have to head off soon to retrieve him. This was for two reasons: partly to relieve them of the responsibility of looking after sixty pounds of canine bone and muscle, and partly before the ever-hungry Labrador ate himself to death. Although his 'I'm starving' act no longer worked on me, Lina fell for it every time and he always came back from a visit to them a good bit heavier than when he went.

I bade farewell to the pair of elderly gentlemen who had been giving me an interesting, if slightly repetitive, treatise on the joys of fly fishing, and went across to where Anna was standing with her sister and a handful of other relatives, listening to Zia Menca outlining the gist of her next blog post. It came as no surprise to learn that this was to be her investigation into attempts by a pharmaceutical firm to hide the fact that their latest drug had the unfortunate side effect of producing temporary blindness. The title of her blog was *VERITAS ITALICA* – Italian Truth – and, from what Anna had told me, her aunt lived and breathed conspiracy theories, corruption in high places, supernatural phenomena and the unexplained and the underhand in general.

The Italian police and armed forces regularly came under her scrutiny and she had been suspicious of me at first until I had convinced her that I really had retired from my former job as a detective at Scotland Yard. It had taken time and a couple of good meals in the local restaurant before she had relented and accepted me into the bosom of the family. Now as she saw me, she reached out with an arthritic hand and gripped my arm remarkably firmly.

'What do you think we should do, Chief Inspector?' She always called me by my former rank but it was out of affection – or at least I hoped so. She spoke very clearly and I found her easy to understand. By now, I was used to the way the Tuscans speak Italian and I had even been told I was beginning to sound like one of them myself.

'What to do about what, Zia Menca?'

'About unscrupulous pharmaceutical companies putting profit over morality?'

I grinned at her. 'Bring back the death penalty and hang the lot of them?'

I saw an answering spark in her bright old eyes. 'Not such a bad idea after all, but maybe just a trifle too radical, even for a police officer.'

'An *ex*-police officer; I'm a private investigator these days, remember. Well, alternatively, if you don't want to hang them, then why not make them take their own drugs for a few months and that way they can experience the side effects for themselves. I imagine that being rendered temporarily blind might help them get the point.'

'Excellent idea, I'll propose it.'

I stood and chatted for another few minutes until it really was time to leave. After thanking her for the party and wishing her well, Anna and I kissed her goodbye and made our way out, kissing and shaking hands with all manner of other guests here in the *sala communale* as we did so. It looked as though most of the village had turned out and I was pleased for Zia Menca. She deserved her celebrity.

The drive back to Virgilio and Lina's house on the outskirts of Florence took less than twenty minutes and we found them still sitting outside in the garden, enjoying the heat of the unusually warm weather for early May with Oscar sprawled before them with a satisfied look on his face and a bulging tummy. He did, at least, have the decency to get to his feet and come over to say hello when he saw us. I ruffled his ears and shot a mock-accusing glance at Lina.

'What part of, "I've already fed him, don't give him anything else," didn't you understand, Lina?' I gave her a big smile. She and I got on really well and she had been working for me now for almost a month as my receptionist, secretary, personal assistant, researcher, occasional dog walker and general office manager, and she had taken a massive amount of weight off my shoulders.

She smiled back. 'I only gave him a few bits and pieces, honest. He looked so hungry...'

Her husband waved towards the cool box alongside the table. 'Cold beers or cold water if you want it. Help yourselves, or would you like a coffee? Come and talk about anything but work.' Virgilio was an inspector in the Florence murder squad and he often put work my way. I was very grateful to him for this and, in fact, he had been instrumental in suggesting that I set up my own investigative agency last year.

I headed for the beer. 'Work, what's that?' I gave him a grin. 'Now that I have my wonderful new PA, I'm a lot freer than I was. This is actually a relatively quiet time of year for me, but I doubt whether that'll last.'

The winter had been a busy mix of unfaithful husbands, bored housewives, pilfering home helps and missing persons – and, memorably, a missing tortoise called Walter – interspersed with a few days helping Virgilio and his team with cases where English speakers were involved. I grabbed a cold beer for myself and indicated the cool box to Anna, who shook her head and sat down beside Lina. I took a seat alongside her and Oscar slumped down between us.

Anna gave a little sigh. 'I'm happy for you, Dan. Unlike you, this is *my* busiest time of the year. With exam season coming up, most of my students are paranoid, and I hardly have a minute to myself.' Anna was a lecturer in medieval and Renaissance history at the University of Florence and she took her job very seriously.

Just at that moment, my phone started ringing and I saw that it was Paul in London.

Inspector Paul Wilson and I had worked together for almost

twenty years at Scotland Yard before I had taken early retirement two years ago and he was one of my best friends.

'Hi, Paul, how's life?'

'Hi, Dan.' He sounded a bit subdued, embarrassed even. 'I'm fine, thanks, but I was hoping you could help me.'

He often did me favours when I had queries about cases with links to the UK so I knew I would be only too glad if I could to repay his kindness. 'Anything I can do, just say the word. What's the trouble?'

'Have you ever come across any ufologists?'

For a moment, I struggled with the unfamiliar word. 'Ufologists?'

'People who're interested in UFOs; you know, alien life, little green men, flying saucers, that sort of thing. Ring any bells with you?'

'I've never had direct dealings with anybody like that, but I imagine there are quite a few of them about these days. No doubt they would have appreciated *Return of the Scaly Things from the Other World* or whatever it was called.'

'Sorry, what?'

'Just a crappy B-movie I was watching the other night. Anyway, I've never knowingly met a ufologist, although I did like the woman with the red hair in *The X Files*. What's up? Don't tell me aliens have landed.'

'Who knows? It's Sandra... my little sister. Do you remember her? She's in a spot of bother.'

I vaguely remembered Paul's sister as a gangly fourteen- or fifteen-year-old with braces on her teeth. I had met her quite a few years ago so she must have grown up by now. 'Yes. I remember Sandra. What's the trouble?'

'I've just had my mother on the phone and then a long talk with Sandra herself, crying her eyes out. She went over to Italy on holiday a few days ago with a girlfriend and a bunch of UFO hunters, and one of the group's been killed.'

'Killed, how?' Inevitably, given my background, I immediately found myself wondering if the death had been suspicious. Was this why Paul was asking for my help?

'There was a fire a couple of hours ago and they found the guy's body in the ashes.'

'Accident or murder?'

'Sandra's convinced it was murder, but the police up there aren't so sure. From what she says, they're still trying to make up their minds if it might have been an accident. Apparently, the group have all been told they have to stay put for now or she says she'd be on her way home like a shot. She's really not into the UFO thing and was only there to show willing for her friend, Maggie. She doesn't know anybody else and she's scared stiff at the thought that there might be a killer among them.'

'When you say, "up there", whereabouts is "up there"?'

'Right up in the north of Italy, in the Alps.' There was a pause while he checked his notes. 'The Aosta Valley, apparently; do you know where that is?'

I knew exactly where this was, because each time I drive to or from the UK, I usually go through the Mont Blanc tunnel through the Alps into France, and that's at the top end of the Aosta Valley. I had a feeling I knew what Paul wanted to ask me, so I saved him the trouble. 'Do you want me to pop up there and take a look?' It was the least I could do.

There was relief in his voice when he replied. 'That would be amazing, but can you spare the time? Isn't it miles away from where you are?'

It was about four or five hours away from Florence but I played down the distance. 'A few hours' drive, no biggie. Give me the details.'

I pulled out my ever-present notebook – old habits die hard – and scribbled down the directions. It sounded as though the ufologist encampment consisting of a mixture of mobile homes, caravans and tents was high up in the mountains, no doubt in a remote spot, which would make it quite a good location for a murder. I told him I'd check my diary and call him back but I knew I owed it to him to get up there as soon as possible. Once he'd given me the details, I queried if he had any other information.

'If it really was murder, what about motive? Any idea who the victim is and whether anybody there might have a reason for wanting him dead?'

'She doesn't know very much. It's only just happened and there's no formal identification yet – the body was too badly burned – but Sandra says the group up there believe it to be a guy called Nick Green. They think he was in his late forties or early fifties but no one knew him particularly well.'

'And he was British?'

'That's what Sandra says. Apparently, the group's almost exclusively made up of Brits. The problem is that he was travelling on his own and nobody there knew him. I imagine his documents may well have been burned in the fire so I expect it'll take a while to find out for sure who he was. The thing is, she says it's a weird set-up and she doesn't trust any of them very much. Some of them appear to be very tight-lipped about what happened. She says it's almost as if there's a conspiracy of silence.'

I mulled this over as I sipped my beer and an idea occurred to me. 'I was just thinking, if there *is* something dodgy going on and I pitch up there announcing myself as a private detective, the odds are that they'll just clam up. What about if I go up there incognito, pretending to be a UFO fanatic, and see if I can join in with the ufologists? That way I might be able to wriggle my way into their confidence.'

There was a pause while Paul gave it some thought. 'That's not a bad idea. And you could probably help out with the interpreting by stepping forward and offering your services, further ingratiating yourself with the group. Sandra says half the problem is that none of them speak more than a few words of Italian, so communication with the police isn't easy. I suppose the question is whether you reckon you could convince them that you have an all-consuming interest in extra-terrestrial life in order to be accepted. Could you do that?'

I looked up at the sky above my head. The candles on the table prevented me from seeing much but on a clear night like this, I knew it would be a mass of twinkling stars. Whether there were other life forms out there remained unproven for now and I'd never subscribed to it. Although the idea of visitors from outer space seemed as unlikely to me as Oscar giving up food, my parents had brought me up to respect other people's beliefs – however wacky they might sound to me. I felt sure I would be able to suspend my disbelief in order to fit in. I'd been reading up on the sky at night recently and had even bought myself a star atlas so as to help in identifying what I was seeing on my evening walks with Oscar. As a result, I felt I could probably put up a reasonably convincing act if pushed.

'I don't see why not. And my van should fit in with the less flashy ones quite nicely.' My van is a nine-year-old VW with seats that fold down to give a flat sleeping area – although it occurred to me that I would have to share it with Oscar and I knew from experience that that promised to be challenging. 'I just hope the little green men don't mind me bringing my dog.'

When the call ended, I gave the others a summary of what Paul had just told me and I looked across at Anna. Things were going really well between us now and we had been going out for over six months. 'What do you think, sweetheart? Do you feel like going out and buying yourself an *ET* T-shirt and coming with me to meet the visitors from another world – that's the ufologists I'm talking about?'

She gave me what my mother would have called an old-fashioned look. 'Would I like to come and spend two or three days in the freezing cold mountains sleeping in the back of a van with two snorers – and at least one of them with flatulence – and spend the daytime mingling with a bunch of deluded loonies? No toilet, no shower, no privacy, no, I can't think of anything worse.' To soften the blow, she reached across and caught hold of my hand. 'You know I love spending time with you and Oscar, *carissimo*, but even if I wanted to come, I can't get away. I'll be tied up with lectures and seminars every day this week.'

I gave her hand a little squeeze in return. 'You're a very wise woman. I'm prepared to accept that we may not be alone in the universe, but I'm having serious reservations about sharing the van with Oscar.'

Virgilio, as always, was very supportive and he offered some practical assistance. 'Depending on where the encampment is, it'll probably be within the jurisdiction of the *squadra mobile* in Aosta. I have a good friend up there. I'll give him a call now and see what I can find out.' He glanced at his watch. 'It's late now so I may have to wait to speak to him until the morning. If I get hold of him, I'll tell him who you are and say that you're happy to help out if required. Okay?' He reached for his phone.

I thanked him and sipped my beer as I talked it over with Lina. Today was Tuesday and we worked out that there was nothing particularly pressing in my diary for the rest of the week so that should give me ample time to drive up next morning and spend three or four nights up in the Alps. Hopefully, things would be resolved by the weekend and I would be able to leave and come home. In fact, the idea of a few days in the high mountains sounded rather appealing – and I felt sure Oscar would agree with me. I called Paul back and told him I hoped to be there around lunchtime next day and he was very grateful. He said he had told Sandra that I would be coming, and she had sounded most relieved. As agreed, he had also told her not to mention my true identity to anybody up there for now.

My call to Paul finished at almost the same time as Virgilio got off the phone to his pal in Aosta. 'Right, Pierre tells me there's been a development.'

'Pierre? Is he French?'

'No, Italian; the Aosta Valley's what's called an autonomous region. Many of the people there are bilingual: French and Italian, or trilingual, I should say – many of the locals speak patois, which is a mixture of both languages. Come to think of it, I seem to remember reading that there's one of the valleys where they even speak German so it's a real mixture. Pierre is Inspector Pierre Gressan and he was born and bred up there. He's checked the file and he tells me the body was found at nine-fifteen tonight – so less than two hours ago. It was seriously burnt and the first impression was of a tragic accident, but the paramedics who attended discovered that the side of the skull had been smashed in. They say it's impossible to tell at the moment whether that was done accidentally or whether somebody deliberately hit him over the head with a heavy object. The body has been removed to the mortuary and the pathologist has promised to produce a preliminary report tomorrow morning, but it could well be that this was no accident. The site where the body was found has been cordoned off and the *Carabinieri* are mounting guard for tonight. If the doctor confirms it was definitely foul play, the murder team will go up there tomorrow and start questioning everybody.'

'What did he say when you told him I was coming up there pretending to be one of the ufologists?'

'He said it sounded like a good plan but he told me it's not his case. It's being handled by an Inspector Costey, who'll be in charge, but Pierre says he'll make sure they all get the word that you're coming so you don't get held up.'

I thanked him most warmly and glanced down at the Labrador who was still sprawled at my feet. 'Well, Oscar, so how do you feel about doing a bit of sniffing about in the Alps?'

He glanced up for a second or two and wagged the end of his tail lazily. Sniffing about was sniffing about. He didn't mind where he did it.

2

WEDNESDAY MORNING

Before going to bed the previous night, I had studied the map and I felt confident that I knew where I had to go. The drive north would begin with the tortuous autostrada towards Bologna through the Apennines. While this road is an engineering triumph with its tunnels and bridges, I knew that it would no doubt be packed with heavy goods vehicles crawling along in the slow lane. Still, I owed it to Paul to do him this favour and a few days in the mountains promised to make a pleasant change.

After a decent walk for Oscar and a substantial breakfast for me – naturally with the bacon rind going to the Labrador – we set off at just after eight. It wasn't a bad drive and by midday, the Alps were clearly visible ahead of us. The motorway, which had been running across the flatlands of the River Po, passed the little town of Ivrea and entered the steep-sided Aosta Valley. For somebody used to the rolling hills and valleys of England or, indeed, of Tuscany, this was alien territory – although not necessarily in a little green men sense.

These foothills of the Alps would have qualified as mountains in Britain and the tops were thousands of feet above me. Signs at the side of the road confirmed that this was a proudly autonomous region just as Virgilio had said and I immediately started to see French place names on the road signs. After passing a place called Pont Saint-Martin, I came to Châtillon and here I turned off the autostrada and started climbing more steeply on a narrow, winding road signposted Cervinia.

As we climbed, the scenery became ever more rugged and forbidding. Although it was early May, the tops of the hills were still dusted with white and the higher peaks ahead of me looked as though they were metres deep in eternal snows. The houses we passed were now unmistakably Alpine; the older ones predominantly stone and most of them with carved wooden balconies, many of which were hung with troughs containing brightly coloured geraniums and other flowers whose names escape me – I've never been great at names of plants.

I stopped just before reaching Valtournenche, which I knew to be the place where I had to turn right off the main road and start the steeper climb up to the ufologists' camp. As far as I could judge, I was now probably only about five or six kilometres from my destination as the crow – or up there, more probably the eagle – flies, although I knew that it was over a thousand metres further up the side of the valley. No doubt getting there would involve quite a few more kilometres of twisting road and would take some time, so a break for Oscar and for myself seemed sensible. A track led into a wood and I set off along it to stretch my legs. Even though it was lunchtime, it was noticeably cooler up here than it had been even first thing this morning in Tuscany, and I had a feeling Anna had been dead right about the likelihood of the nights being chilly up here.

After a walk for Oscar and a comfort break in the trees for both of us, I went into the nearby Café de la Paix and ordered a croque monsieur. The café itself, in spite of its French name, was still recognisably Italian and the barman greeted me in Italian. He was a fit-looking man probably in his mid or late thirties with the tanned skin of an outdoorsman and he was wearing a Salomon ski sweatshirt. In spite of it being almost one o'clock, I was the only customer apart from two elderly gentlemen playing cards at a table in the far corner. I ate my cheesy toast with my dog resting his head on my knee, staring wistfully into my eyes in the hope of arousing some shreds of pity as he clearly felt he was on the brink of starvation. I held firm until the end when I gave him the last bit of the crust. On the walls of the wood-panelled bar were pairs of vintage, wooden skis, snowshoes, photos of local skiing heroes and posters advertising downhill ski races. No prizes for guessing the principal interests of people in this valley, at least in the winter. I asked the barman if the skiing season had finished and he nodded.

'Yes, it was all over by the end of March this year. By the time Easter came, all the snow had melted away – at least at the lower levels.' He glanced out of the window at the green slopes above us with the same wistful expression as Oscar had just produced. 'And, to be honest, it wasn't a great season. We had *rain* in January.' He shook his head in disbelief. 'Rain, when it should have been snow! I've never seen anything like it. The winters are getting warmer and shorter, and the glaciers are melting at a frightening rate. Are you going up to Cervinia?' His accent sounded almost French when he pronounced the letter 'r'. Evidently this was the way the locals spoke up here.

'Probably not today, but I'm sure I will do tomorrow or the next day.'

'Well, when you do get up there, look across to the left of the Cervino. The glacier that used to come to within a few hundred metres of the town is now little more than a rocky scree slope with a stream running through it.'

'Is the Cervino the biggest mountain up here?' I wasn't familiar with the name.

He shook his head. 'The Cervino is the most spectacular and it's a mecca for climbers, but the Monte Rosa alongside it is even higher. There's still skiing up on the glaciers of the Monte Rosa but most of the lower slopes have been green grass for over a month now.' He gave a little sigh. 'Good for the cows and the walkers but no good for the skiers. Have you come here to ski?'

I thought it might be a good idea to test the water to see whether the local bush telegraph had already heard what had happened up there. 'No, I'm not here for the snow. Don't laugh, but I've come because I've heard that there have been reports of extra-terrestrial activity. I'm interested in that sort of thing.' As I said it, I was bracing myself for a hefty shot of ridicule but to my surprise, he appeared not to share my scepticism.

'It's downright creepy. Friends up the hill say they've seen lights in the sky at night and I've just heard this morning that the aliens have killed somebody.'

I did my best to conceal my surprise that he knew so much and decided to plead ignorance for now. 'Killed? Do you mean the aliens have landed?'

He shook his head and smiled. 'I hope not. I just heard a couple of hours ago from a friend whose sister lives up at Chamois. She said it happened just above Montaz, which isn't far from here.' I recognised the place name I had been given as the site of the ufologists' camp. 'The police and *Carabinieri* have gone up there in force this morning so something bad must have happened.' ·

Back in the car, I checked my messages and found one from Paul.

It was murder. I'm sure they'll tell you when you get there but Sandra has just been in touch to say that the police are now

treating it as murder. The UFO people are getting very excited.
Checkout their website: www.fellowshipoforb.com

I clicked the link and this led me to the website and the Facebook page of a ufologist group who went by the rather corny-
sounding name of the Fellowship of the Silver Orb. It appeared
that this was the group who had organised this flying-saucer hunt
up here in the Alps this spring. As far as I could discover, these
sorts of gatherings were a regular event for the group, but this
appeared to be the first time the ufologists had ventured into Italy.
The fellowship's website provided no address for correspondence
but, by reading through the names of the contributors to the newsletter and doing a bit of elementary detective work, it was fairly
clear that the moving spirits behind it were based somewhere in
the UK.

Their Facebook feed was filled with photos of some very beautiful Alpine scenery and some indistinct lights in the night sky,
which were so small, they could have been anything from fireflies
to distant aircraft or even the International Space Station. The
most recent post – posted barely ten minutes earlier – was far more
sensationalist:

Tragedy strikes. Man killed by alien spacecraft. The time has
come. Full details to follow.

This was displayed beneath a colourful poster of the star-
studded night sky boasting:

WE KNOW THE TRUTH

It didn't go so far as to say *we told you so* but the implication was
clear.

As I had expected, the route up from Valtournenche to the ufologists' camp involved no fewer than twelve hairpin bends and countless other sharp corners. Around three quarters of the way up, I drove through a little village of not more than a couple of dozen houses but where I was surprised to see a hotel with a bar/restaurant. This was a pleasant bonus. If I ran into trouble cohabiting with Oscar in the van, I could always try it, either for meals or for a bed and a hot shower – as long as they were prepared to let Oscar share my room with me.

The road continued to climb for another kilometre or two and, as we gained height, the views became ever more spectacular. My attention was particularly drawn to the cluster of the highest peaks at the head of the valley and to one in particular. This mountain was an absolutely massive bare chunk of rock like a narrow pyramid thousands of feet high, whose summit was shrouded in cloud. Although the sides in places were vertical, even from here I could see that all the horizontal surfaces were covered in snow. Presumably, this was the Cervino that the barista had referred to and I was surprised I hadn't heard of such an imposing mountain. It looked vaguely familiar and I couldn't understand why the name meant nothing to me. Mind you, I freely acknowledge that I'm not that great at geography.

I followed the increasingly narrow road and a few minutes later, passed a sign indicating the presence of a café hidden in the trees to the right. I made a mental note that this would be handy for my regular caffeine fix. Clearly, it wasn't quite as deserted up here as I had been expecting. Shortly after this, the road finally deteriorated from grey tarmac into a rough track and here I found myself confronted by a roadblock. A blue and white police car was parked there and two cones had been placed across the entrance to the track. A young police officer opened the squad-car door and climbed out, holding up his hand to stop me. I did as requested and opened my window as he approached. He addressed me politely, but firmly.

'I'm afraid you can't go any further. This road is closed to vehicles and pedestrians alike. It's now a crime scene.'

'Thank you, Officer, but I'm expected.' I produced my ID and held it out to him. 'My name's Armstrong, and *Commissario* Gressan told me he'd let you know I was coming.'

He glanced down at his clipboard and nodded. 'Yes, of course, *Commissario* Armstrong. Go straight on up the track and you'll find my colleagues. I'll get a message to Inspector Costey to say that you're on your way.'

It didn't surprise me that Virgilio and his buddy had chosen to give me a police rank, even though it was almost two years now since I had said goodbye to life as a chief inspector. It certainly appeared to do the trick here, and the officer gave me a smart salute before hurrying across to remove the cones.

My ageing VW minibus didn't have four-wheel drive but over the winter it had proved itself capable of coping with most road surfaces including mud and even a sprinkling of Tuscan snow, and it took the potholes and gravel in its stride. By now, Oscar had realised that we were approaching the end of our long drive and he was standing in the boot peering about with interest, his tail beginning to wag in anticipation. The track curled up through a dense pine forest until it emerged into a wide, open area of relatively flat Alpine pasture dotted with clumps of wild flowers and bordered on three sides by steep mountain slopes. A hundred years ago, this would have been empty but for a handful of cows grazing on the lush spring pasture, but today the scene was very different.

Three police cars, a minivan and a dark blue *Carabinieri* Land Rover were parked up there, and beyond them was the ufologists' encampment. There were fewer vehicles than I had been expecting: barely a dozen campervans – many of them a whole lot more battered even than mine – spread out around the flat area, and a large tent had been erected over to one side of them. Apart from a mountain stream, I could see no sign of washing facilities or showers, so presumably personal hygiene took second place to alien encounters as far as many of these seekers after the truth were concerned. I thought it best not to dwell too long on the absence of toilet facilities either. What's that thing they say about bears in the woods?

The exception was a shiny motorhome, noticeably larger and newer than any of the others. This was parked on its own on the far side of the encampment and there was an area of no man's land between it and the run-of-the-mill ufologists. It was clear that the occupants of this luxury accommodation liked their privacy. I wondered who they might be.

A quick look around at the others confirmed that I had brought the perfect vehicle if I wanted to fit in with the rank-and-file ufologists. Almost all of the vehicles were British registered campervans. Some were venerable antiques and a couple of them amazed me that they had been able to make the long journey without giving up the ghost. One had what looked like some sort of radar scanner tied rather precariously onto the roof rack and another boasted a large telescope set up alongside it. Smoke was coming from a campfire roughly in the centre of the camp and I could see figures sitting around it. I glanced over my shoulder at Oscar.

'Here we go. We're approaching UFO territory.'

From the expression on his face, he didn't believe in them any more than I did… but they might have food.

3

WEDNESDAY AFTERNOON

I could feel eyes on me as I bumped across the rough, grassy terrain until I found a flattish spot as far away from the stream as possible. I knew my dog of old – show him a puddle, pond, pool, lake or river and he'll jump right in, and being in the company of a damp, smelly dog probably wouldn't be my best introduction to the group. I turned off the engine and this was the signal for Oscar's tail to start wagging more excitedly. I saw his black face in the mirror, white teeth gleaming, looking at me with anticipation – UFOs or no UFOs – so I climbed out and went around to open the door for him. He jumped out onto the straggly grass and shook himself, nostrils flared, and I wagged my finger at him.

'Stay out of the water. *Capito?*'

He adopted his butter-wouldn't-melt-in-his-mouth look but then turned away as he saw that we had company and his tail started wagging even more vigorously.

'What a lovely dog. What's his name?' It was a woman's voice and I glanced around to find myself being approached by a very good-looking, young woman with immaculate hair and make-up in spite of the circumstances. I'm no expert on female fashion but even I could see that the clothes she was wearing – a pink linen top and white jeans – hadn't come off a supermarket shelf. She was probably not much older than thirty and she looked gorgeous, definitely not what I had been expecting. I found it remarkably easy to produce a smile for her.

'Hi, I'm Dan and this is Oscar. Oscar, come and say hello to your new friend.'

'Hi, Dan. I'm Libby.'

She sounded friendly, although there was a lacklustre note to her voice, probably as a result of what had happened. She was quite tall and she had to crouch down to make a fuss of the Labrador. I murmured a silent prayer that he wouldn't climb all over her white jeans. I could almost hear Anna's voice saying in disbelief, *White jeans up here?*

Libby held Oscar's head between both hands and gave him a sizzling smile. 'And hello, Oscar. Are you a good doggie?'

There was more warmth in her tone as she addressed him, but I couldn't blame her for that. He's always had a way with the ladies, which is certainly not something I could say about myself. After a few moments, she stood back up again, leaving Oscar lying on his back, all four paws in the air, wagging his tail and clearly relishing the attention.

'Are you here for the encounters as well, Dan?'

Luckily, I now knew what she was talking about. The word had cropped up regularly on the group's Facebook page so I was able to answer confidently.

'I sincerely hope so.' Deciding I might as well start digging, I tried a direct question. 'Have you had any close encounters with alien life?'

She shook her head with an expression of regret on her face but, deep down, I wasn't totally convinced. Call it an old copper's hunch but I wasn't sure she was as interested as all that. 'I wish…'

But then she rallied. 'But I have seen the lights in the sky up here on three nights now.'

Of course, lights in the sky could be anything. Geneva and the Alps are situated below one of the main air corridors between north and south Europe and a jet full of people ten miles up might easily be confused with something extraterrestrial – at least by people with a vested interest in that sort of thing. I bottled up a fair shot of scepticism and just gave her a little smile.

The sound of approaching footsteps attracted my attention and I glanced around to see a woman maybe in her late thirties or early forties with a mass of long, dark hair. I gave her a smile and was rewarded by a hint of a smile in return. She was looking as frazzled as Libby and certainly anything but relaxed.

'Who're your new friends, Libby?' Her accent was unmistakably London, or at least the south-east.

'This is Dan. He's come to join us. And this is Oscar.'

I held out my hand. 'Hi, I'm pleased to meet you.'

'Hi, Dan.' She stretched out an unexpectedly elegant, manicured hand and shook mine before immediately transferring her attention to my dog. Over the almost two years that he and I had cohabited, I had got used to this by now. It happened a lot but I didn't blame her. He *is* a lot better looking than I am.

After making a fuss of him, she stood up and addressed me. 'My name's Alice. Is this your first time up here?'

I nodded. 'That's right, I'm a newbie. I live in Italy and when I discovered that you were all going to be here, I knew I wanted to join in.'

'Well, I'm afraid you've chosen a terrible time to come. We had the most awful tragedy here yesterday.' From the dark rings beneath her eyes, she probably hadn't had much sleep since hearing the news.

I affected an innocent air. 'Tragedy? What happened? Is that what the police are doing here?'

'Yes, one of the group was killed last night. The whole place has been sealed off since late last night. Did you have trouble getting through the police roadblock? I had a heck of an argument this morning – or I would have done if we'd been able to understand each other.'

'I had to do a lot of explaining but thankfully, I speak Italian and they let me through in the end. Have you just arrived as well?'

She shook her head. 'No, I'm staying at the hotel just a few kilometres down the hill.' She managed to produce a hint of a smile. 'So's Libby. Neither of us are the camping type.'

Libby gave a theatrical shudder and I nodded to myself: a hotel room explained the white jeans. I returned to the murder. 'Somebody was killed? What happened?'

Alice answered. 'It was a guy called Nick. He'd only just joined us up here. As for what happened, the police say he may have been murdered, but we don't have any details.' There was something in her voice that didn't quite ring true and I had a feeling she maybe did know more than she was letting on. Might this be what Paul's sister, Sandra, had meant when she had told her brother she thought something funny might be going on? I made no comment and let Alice continue. 'We're still trying to come to terms with it. Julian knows more than I do. Come and let me introduce you to everybody.'

At the mention of the name Julian, I felt sure I saw a cloud pass across Libby's face and she pointed vaguely across towards a clump of trees in the distance. 'You go on. I said I'd go and look for some more firewood.'

I filed that reaction away for future reference and accompanied Alice towards the fire. Oscar trotted along with his tail still wagging. He was in the company of a member of the opposite sex, after all. I queried the name Alice had just used. 'Julian?' In fact, I felt sure I knew who he was. Julian Goodfellow's name had appeared all over the Fellowship of the Silver Orb website and blog, although I'd been unable to find any specific title assigned to him. 'Is he the leader of the group?'

'Yes, although Julian insists we don't have leaders. According to him, we're all leaders... or rather, we're all followers of the visitors.' Although Alice recited this in a serious tone, I had a feeling she maybe wasn't quite as convinced as all that either. Libby had also sounded a bit flaky and Paul had told me that his sister wasn't a convert, so were any of the group true UFO aficionados?

'The visitors?'

'That's what Julian calls them, but he says they aren't really so much visitors as our creators.'

This was getting a bit too esoteric for me. 'What, sort of like God?'

'He told us not to use that word. He says that the visitors chose this planet for us and populated it with our forefathers and mothers. According to Julian, they come down from time to time to check up on our progress.' For a moment, I definitely thought I heard a sceptical note in her voice. My suspicion that she maybe wasn't a totally committed ufologist grew stronger.

'Down from where?'

In response, she pointed skywards with her thumb. 'Up there. Nobody knows where.'

'And you believe that...?' I had to struggle to avoid adding, *load of crap.*

There was a momentary hesitation before she replied. 'That's why I'm here.'

I noted that she hadn't answered my question but I decided that was her own affair. I was a fine one to talk. Still, I did my best to stay in character. 'I imagine we're a great disappointment to our alien creators. Look at the way we're destroying the planet and ourselves.'

'Too true, Dan, too true.'

'Is Julian one of the "visitors"?'

'No, he says he's just an acolyte like we all are. That's him over there.'

She pointed at the group around the campfire and we started walking towards them. She glanced across at me as we did so.

'Do you have experiences of your own?'

'You mean UFO sightings?' I'd been preparing for this line of questioning in the van on the way here. 'I've seen lights in the sky a few times near where I live, but nothing concrete. I live in hope. What about you?'

'Afraid not. As far as I know, of the people here, only Julian has actually seen the visitors.'

'Really?' I did my best to keep the scepticism out of my voice. I wondered where and when his close encounter had taken place. Had he maybe shared a cup of coffee together with an ET looka-like? That would have made the other customers sit up and take notice. Wisely, I chose not to display my cynicism.

As we approached the campfire, a man stood up and produced a grimace that might have been a weak attempt at a smile. He looked understandably downbeat but friendly enough.

'Welcome. Have you come to join us?'

He was probably in his late forties, early fifties – so only a few years younger than me – and, like the two ladies I had just met, he wasn't what I'd been expecting either. If asked, I would have had to admit that I had pictured UFO fanatics as having wild, unruly hair, an earring or two, thick, pebble glasses and crazy, staring eyes. Of course, maybe I'd just watched too much TV. So far, I had seen two attractive and, above all, normal-looking women and now this guy who looked as if he'd just stepped off a Hollywood movie set.

He was tall, with chiselled features, a perfectly trimmed moustache and styled, chestnut-brown hair, just greying at the temples. If the crocodile logo on the immaculate polo shirt he was wearing and the gold of the thin chain just visible around his neck were authentic, he wasn't short of money. From his upper-class accent, it wouldn't have surprised me to hear that he'd been an officer in the Guards or similar. Even with the worry lines on his face and the dark rings under his eyes, he was still a very handsome guy.

I held out my hand in greeting. 'I'd love to join you for a few days if you'll have me. My name's Dan Armstrong. I've just been telling Alice that I live in Italy now and when I saw on Facebook that you were all here, I knew I just had to come along. I'm afraid Alice's just given me the awful news about the death of your friend.'

'I'm pleased to meet you, Dan. I'm Julian Goodfellow. Yes, it's not the best of days, I'm afraid.' He was being very British and stiff-upper-lippish but underneath, he looked and sounded on edge – but murder does that to people. 'We're all still trying to come to terms with what happened to Nick last night.'

I took a chance. 'What did happen to him?'

He just shook his head. 'We're still trying to get our heads around it... Poor Nick.' Clearly, he didn't feel like talking about it. At least for now.

He gave my hand a firm shake and I could feel his eyes on me for a few moments. I braced myself for an inquisition about why I was here, my background and what I did for a living but, to my surprise, he just waved vaguely towards the other people perched on logs and rocks around the fire and raised his voice a smidgen. 'People, this is Dan. He's come to join us.'

A few muted greetings came back, but very few smiles or waves under the circumstances. I counted eleven of them and they looked like a nice enough bunch, although one young couple –

probably only in their early twenties – didn't even glance up. From the expressions on the faces of these two, it was hard to tell if this was because of grief or maybe because they were in the middle of a major row about something. Over to one side were two young women sitting on a log and I thought I intercepted a tiny nod of recognition as the taller of the two caught my eye. I realised that this must be Paul's sister, Sandra, and thought I recognised her, but she had certainly changed since I had last seen her. She was probably in her early twenties now and all traces of the gangly teenager had disappeared. I just gave her and her friend a vague wave and left it at that. Paul and I had agreed that I would keep my identity secret from the group and to do that, we had thought it best if I didn't announce that Sandra and I already knew each other.

In the meantime, Oscar wandered amiably around the group, nudging people with his nose and receiving pats and strokes in return. He even managed to raise a few smiles.

'Hello, Dan. I'm Val. Have you had lunch? Would you like a mug of tea?'

The offer came from a friendly, red-faced lady who was probably around my age, and from her accent, she came from Essex or somewhere to the right of London. Anticipating my acceptance, she reached forward, donned a singed oven glove that had probably started life pink and lifted a smoke-blackened kettle off the glowing embers. 'Milk, sugar?'

'I had a snack down in the valley but I'd love a cuppa. Just milk, please, if you've got any. If not, I bought fresh milk on my way up here this morning.'

'Don't worry, we've got everything here.' She turned to the young woman beside her. 'Millie, be a dear and get the milk, would you? Anybody else want tea?'

Obligingly, the other woman got up and went over to the edge of the little stream, which was evidently acting as an open-air refrigerator, and I gave Oscar a stern look and tut-tutted as he appeared on the point of following her to the water. Grudgingly, he obeyed. Millie lifted a bottle from the shallows where it had been resting and brought it back. Val added milk to a fresh mug for me as well as to her own before filling them with tea from the kettle with a practised hand and passing one across to me. 'Don't worry, it hasn't been stewing since daybreak. I made it fresh only a few minutes before you arrived.'

I thanked her and sat down on a nearby boulder to sip the boiling brew. It was very good. As always, a mug of tea took my mind back to countless occasions in the past when a hot cuppa had cheered me in the course of long surveillance operations. You can't beat it and, unlike coffee, it doesn't produce a smell that can travel hundreds of yards and reach the nostrils of the people under observation. I found myself idly wondering what medieval British policemen did before the arrival of tea on our shores. I seemed to remember reading that people in those days had worked out that water could contain impurities and end up killing them, even if they didn't know why. As a result, most people in medieval Britain drank beer – the fermentation killed most germs – so probably the police, along with much of the population, would have been permanently plastered. Lucky there were no cars on the roads back then.

As I drank my tea, I chatted to Val and Millie and deliberately steered clear of what they believed to have happened to 'poor' Nick. There would be time for that once I had gained their trust. Val told me that Millie was her daughter and that both of them shared a fascination with extra-terrestrial life. This was their annual holiday. For her part, Millie said very little and let her mum do the talking.

On the other side of the fire, Julian had resumed his seat along-side a hard-faced woman who sat stiffly to attention, her eyes fixed on the flames. It came as no surprise to see that these two weren't sitting on rocks or logs but had brought a pair of comfortable-looking folding chairs. The woman was probably around Julian's age and good-looking, but in a frosty, unapproachable sort of way. I wondered if she was his partner or maybe his wife. What appeared clear was that she, like the others, was still feeling the effects of what had happened last night. This came as no surprise to me. Discovering that somebody you knew has been killed can have a seriously upsetting effect on most people.

Apart from them, there were two younger men sitting side by side on a tree trunk and they, at least, corresponded far more closely to my preconceived ideas about how UFO aficionados should look. The plumper of the two, introduced as Geoffrey, was clad in shorts and a stained *Star Wars* T-shirt that looked as though it had been in a death struggle with a tin of baked beans – and had lost. Beside him was a scrawny-looking young man with thick, black-framed glasses whose circular lenses made it look as if he was peering through binoculars. Like his bigger friend, this man, who told me his name was Crispin, was wearing shorts and a slightly less scruffy blue Superman T-shirt and one of those waist-coat things that photographers use with all the pockets. These were stuffed with so many bits and pieces that any shape the garment might once have had had long since been eradicated. It hung from his bony shoulders like a couple of poorly packed shopping bags.

Alice had taken a seat on a rock on her own just along from them and I took a surreptitious look at her. Like Libby, she was immaculately turned out, and I wondered if she was really so deeply into the whole UFO thing as all that. Somehow, she looked out of place in this rustic environment and I wondered how she had ended up in such eccentric company.

A few minutes later, Libby returned with an armful of firewood

and set it down near Val, who thanked her and offered her a mug
of tea, but Libby shook her head.

'Thanks, but I'm fasting today.' She caught my eye and offered
a word of explanation. 'Got to stay in shape for the cameras.'

I indicated that there was space on the rock alongside me and
she sat down – after first making sure she wiped any moss or dirt
off it so as not to dirty the white jeans – and stroked Oscar's head
as he leant happily against her legs. As she did so, I caught a look
from Julian that my dog would have recognised. It was as territorial
as when Oscar goes around peeing on all the trees in an area to
mark what he sees as his preserve. To my suspicious mind, it
looked as though Julian, despite the fact that he was sitting alongside the woman I had pigeonholed as his wife or partner, and
despite probably being twenty years older than Libby, clearly felt
that she belonged to him – to what extent and in what capacity
remained to be seen. I decided it wouldn't do any harm to rock the
boat a little so I gave Libby a big smile and turned on the charm –
insofar as I'm capable of being charming.

'I thought you looked like an actress. Are you famous?'

A little flush of satisfaction flitted across her face. 'Oh no, I'm
just starting out.'

'What sort of acting do you do? Are you in the movies?'

She shook her head. 'TV. I work for Julian's company.'

This was news. 'Julian has a TV company?' I wasn't sure if my
voice would carry across the fire to where Julian and his lady were
sitting so I continued to address myself to Libby. 'What sort of
programmes do you make?'

Julian answered for her. 'We produce documentaries.' Clearly,
he had lynx-like hearing. 'You may have heard of us. The company's called WKTTV. We're one of the best known, if not the best
known, production company specialising in investigations into the
paranormal and, above all, contacts with extra-terrestrial life.'

I hadn't heard of his company but I played along. 'Fantastic. I didn't realise I was in the company of experts in the field. So are you here to make a programme?'

My flattery had the desired effect and I saw him smile. 'We are indeed. As soon as I heard of the recent sightings here in Italy, I knew I just had to come over and I was lucky enough to be able to persuade some like-minded spirits to accompany me.'

I was about to ask him where the Fellowship of the Silver Orb fitted into this scenario when I spotted a couple of police officers emerging from the big tent. This was my opportunity. I looked back across the fire to Julian again. 'I see the police are here. How are you managing with the language? Do they speak English or do you speak Italian?'

He shook his head. 'It's been a nightmare. None of us speak more than a few words of Italian and only one of the police speaks a bit of English, so we're struggling.' I was pleased to see him take the bait. 'Did you say you live here in Italy? Does that mean you speak Italian? If so, you'd be doing us a great service if you could act as interpreter. From what they've told us this morning, they're treating it as murder, but that's ridiculous. We're desperate to know what really happened to Nick and how that affects all of us.'

I jumped to my feet. 'I'd be happy to help out. I'll just go across to speak to those police officers now. From what you're telling me, they'll probably be equally pleased to have a bit of help.'

4

WEDNESDAY AFTERNOON

I walked across to the two officers by the tent and asked if I could
speak to Inspector Costey. The taller of the two indicated that the
inspector was inside so I went into the tent and found a figure in
plain clothes sitting at a trestle table. I approached the table and,
as I did so, three things became immediately apparent. First,
Inspector Costey was a woman, second, she was heavily pregnant,
and third, the expression on her face was anything but welcoming.
Undeterred, I approached the desk and addressed her in Italian.

'Hello, my name's Dan Armstrong. I believe *Commissario*
Gressan told you I was coming.'

'I got the message.' She didn't stand up and she made no move
to shake my hand. Terse and frosty were the first adjectives that
came to mind, but I couldn't blame her. Having a member of the
public – all right, a former police officer, but even so – foisted upon
her couldn't be a bundle of laughs. Add to that the fact that I was a
foreigner and I couldn't help but sympathise, so I hastened to pour
a bit of oil on potentially troubled waters.

'I'm here to help, that's all, Inspector Costey. I've been living
in Italy for a couple of years now and I'm happy to help with any

language problems you might encounter with all these English speakers, but I don't want to get under your feet.' I used the formal form of the pronoun 'you' when I addressed her, rather than the more familiar form. From the look of her, I would do well to keep things respectful – at least for now. 'I'm here because a good friend of mine who's a detective inspector at Scotland Yard in London is concerned about his sister. She's one of the ufologists.' I tried to repeat the charm offensive I had produced for Libby outside. 'But don't feel you have to take me up on my offer. I'm more than happy just to join the other ufologists and stay out of your way if that's what you prefer. I used to hate it when other people tried to get involved with my investigations.'

There was silence for a few seconds while she weighed me up, or rather while she weighed any possible benefit of having me around against the potential annoyance of somebody who might start meddling with her case. Oscar, who had been sitting at my side unusually obediently, must have sensed the tension in the atmosphere because he took it upon himself to stand up and wander over to the other side of the desk. I saw him sit down beside the inspector and give her the full big-brown-eyes treatment, normally reserved for when he was begging for food. It appeared to work and I saw her reach down to stroke his head, and her expression softened a fraction. I still couldn't describe it as friendly, but it was certainly less confrontational than her initial reaction to seeing me had been. She continued to fondle Oscar's ears while she addressed me once more.

'I understand from *Commissario* Gressan that you used to be a senior officer in the British police.'

It wasn't exactly a question but I answered it anyway. 'I don't know about "senior". I used to be a detective chief inspector in the Metropolitan police but I've been retired for two years now.' I didn't mention that I had opened my own investigation agency. There would be time for that in due course.

She pointed towards a chair on my side of the desk and I sat down opposite her and waited for her to make the first move. This time, I didn't have so long to wait. When she did reply, it sounded as though she had decided to accept my presence here, not necessarily with open arms, but at least without outright opposition.

'Did Pierre tell you that we now know for sure that it was murder?' Although we were speaking Italian, she pronounced her 'r's in the French way, just like the barista down the hill from here.

'To be honest, I haven't spoken to him directly. It was a good friend of mine from the murder squad in Florence who spoke to him on my behalf. As for it being murder, Inspector Wilson at Scotland Yard told me an hour ago. He heard it from his sister.'

Inspector Costey looked pleased. 'That's good. I must congratulate my sergeant. He speaks a bit of English, but not a lot, and mine is even worse. We've had a long wait for the pathologist's report – the body was in a terrible state – but the word came through midmorning that they're convinced it was murder. I told my sergeant to tell the campers that this is now a murder investigation, but he wasn't too sure that he'd been able to get the message across to everybody. He said they didn't all appear to react very much when they heard the news.'

I caught her eye. 'Maybe it didn't come as such a surprise to some of them after all.'

She nodded. 'My thoughts entirely.'

'Could I ask how the victim was killed?'

'A heavy blow to the side of the head, just above the left ear. The victim's skull was shattered by it.' There was another lengthy pause before she continued. 'Pierre told me you're planning on pretending to be one of the UFO hunters so as to blend in. Is that because you think they might be hiding something?'

'I really don't know. I need to sit down for a quiet talk with my friend's sister first. Her name's Sandra Wilson. She told her brother she's concerned that there's something not quite right here. I think I've identified which one she is and I'll try and get her on her own if that's okay with you. Like I say, the last thing I want to do is to tread on your toes. In the meantime, I've just met the leader, Julian Goodfellow, and I told him I'd come over here now to see if you need any help with translating. Do you?'

This time, her expression did soften a bit. 'We certainly do. I'd like to sit down and interview all of the ufologists.' From the dismissive way she used the word, I got the feeling she was no more convinced about the existence of alien life than I was. 'So, yes, I would be very grateful for your help.'

'Well, I'm happy to assist.'

'What do you want me to call you? Are you using your real name?'

'Yes, I'm Dan Armstrong – but I'm making no mention of my former career and I'm telling people to call me Dan. Please call me whatever you like.'

She nodded and heaved herself to her feet with an effort. From the size of her baby bump, she looked ready to give birth any minute now and I felt sorry for her. Combining pregnancy with such a demanding job couldn't be easy. Oscar, job done, stood up as well and came back around the desk with a satisfied smile on his face. And don't try and tell me that Labradors don't smile. They really do.

Inspector Costey followed him around and held out her hand towards me. 'I'm pleased to meet you, Signor Armstrong.'

She was keeping it formal and that was fine with me. Whether this was because she was still pissed off at having me around or just because she was a formal sort of person was unimportant. I was all in favour as it would further distance me from the investi-

gation and hopefully add to my street cred with the ufologists. We
shook hands and she pointed towards the door.

'Now, in the first instance, I'd like to say a few words to the
group outside, so if you could translate for me that would be a
great help.'

I followed her out and across to the campfire. The ufologists
were all still sitting there and they had been joined by another
member of the group. He was a big, chubby, tough-looking character in a red and black check lumberjack shirt, well-worn jeans
and a battered cowboy hat. With his shaggy black beard, he looked
as if he had just emerged from wrestling grizzly bears in the forests
of the Rocky Mountains. What was interesting was that he was
standing beside a serious-looking video camera mounted on a
tripod and the lens was pointing straight at the inspector and me.

Inspector Costey stepped forward. 'Good morning, my name is
Inspector Carmela Costey from the Aosta police. I would be
grateful if you would avoid filming for now. Thank you.' I translated and, after a glance across at Julian, the cameraman did as
requested. The inspector produced her ID from her pocket and
held it up for them to see. A few people craned their necks but
most of them didn't bother. I translated what it said into English
and saw a bit more interest on their faces, particularly when I got
to the words 'murder squad'. Julian was the first to react.

'How can you be sure that it was murder?' There was a
confrontational note in his voice but I thought I could hear something else as well – maybe fear? If so, of what? Of the police? Fear
that the same thing might happen to him as had happened to Nick
Green or fear of being unmasked as a murderer?

I translated for the benefit of the inspector and I was impressed
at the way she replied. No nonsense. Definitely the way to go. 'Yes,
we're sure it was murder. The pathology lab has assured me that
there can be no doubt about it. Are you the leader here?'

I answered for Julian, keeping it formal. 'That gentleman there is Julian Goodfellow. He's sort of the leader although they don't acknowledge him as such.'

The inspector nodded. 'Thank you. Please tell them that you'll be helping me with the language as I proceed with my enquiries.' I relayed this information and noticed that Alice, Libby, Val and Sandra nodded while the others remained fairly impassive. The inspector continued and I translated as she went along.

'I understand that you're all here because you have an interest in science fiction. Is that correct?'

Bristling, Julian answered for the group. 'Definitely not science *fiction*. We're here because we firmly believe in the existence of extra-terrestrial life.'

The inspector listened to my translation without any visible reaction. 'Please would you ask this gentleman how long he and the group plan on staying here?'

I translated and Julian answered. 'Please tell the inspector that we've been here for three days now and we intend staying until the end of next week, two weeks in total. There's no law against that, is there?' He was doing his best to sound tough but there was still that nervous edge to his voice. 'But, are you completely sure it wasn't an accident?'

I translated as requested but the inspector ignored the question. 'Now, please can you tell me why you've chosen this location?'

'There have been a number of UFO sightings in this area and we decided to come and see for ourselves... but murder?'

'UFO sightings? You mean spaceships?' The inspector ignored the murder question once more and was doing a good job of masking her scepticism about little green men. I decided I rather liked the way Inspector Carmela Costey worked. She was probably in her mid or late thirties, not much older than my own daughter, but she was handling herself like an old pro.

Julian answered automatically. 'Nothing tangible so far, I'm afraid. But we've been seeing regular lights in the sky at night.'

'And last night between eight o'clock and nine-fifteen, did you or any of your companions hear or see anything unexplained?'

'We've been discussing that most of the day. I didn't notice anything myself, but Peter and Bethany saw the fire and heard a roaring sound. They're the ones who found the body and alerted the emergency services.'

'And who are they?'

Julian indicated the morose-looking couple who were following the conversation closely. 'Peter and Bethany are over there.'

They were probably in their early twenties, the girl maybe even younger. She was quite small, with long, fair hair hanging loose around her face, while he was taller but still slim. At a guess, I would have said university students, but what they were doing here and not at lectures was a mystery. Like the others, they probably hadn't had much sleep the previous night and both looked weary as well as bewildered – and little wonder if they had discovered a seriously burnt body the previous night.

'And nobody else saw or heard anything? No vehicles?'

I threw her question out to everybody and saw only shakes of the head. The inspector now decided the time was right to talk in more detail about the murder. As she did so, I studied the faces around me.

'As I've just told you, this is now a murder investigation. The victim was killed or rendered unconscious by a vicious blow to the side of the head. The killer then set fire to the body, presumably to cover his or her tracks.' As I translated, Millie turned pale and her mother, Val, looked little better. Peter and Bethany, the grim couple who had found the body, looked positively green, and the only ones not to look quite so appalled were the two geeky men – no doubt brought up on a diet of violent video games. As far as Julian and his partner were concerned, he had stretched his arm around her and they had turned towards each other so that their faces were hidden from view, so I couldn't assess their reaction.

The inspector continued. 'As a result, my team will be giving the crime scene and its surroundings a close forensic examination so I would ask you all to stay away from that area until instructed otherwise.' She directed her next question at Julian. 'Did you or any of your group know the victim well?'

I translated and Julian, who was looking subdued, shook his head. 'I'm afraid not. He only arrived the day before yesterday. He told me he knew of the fellowship – that's the group to which we all belong – but he wasn't a member, and this was the first time he'd ever been to one of our meets. As for the others, you'd better ask them. You see, the fellowship's a big group but it's all online and I'd only met one or two of the others before coming over to Italy and I imagine it's the same for most of us here. I'm not sure if any of us already knew Nick.'

The inspector asked me to repeat the question to the others to ascertain if any of them had known the victim. We both looked around the assembled group as I translated, but nobody reacted so she returned to the matter in hand. 'I see, so none of you knew him. That's a pity because we're still trying to get confirmation of his identity. I'm afraid we'll need to take statements from each of you so please don't leave this encampment until we've finished making our enquiries. That may well take a number of days. I've stationed some of my officers down at the end of the track to make sure that you all comply with this requirement. Thank you.'

Alice held up her hand. 'Dan, could you tell the inspector that some of us are staying in the hotel down the hill in Montaz? We drive up and down each day. Can she see that the officers at the roadblock are instructed to let us through?'

I passed on the request and Inspector Costey nodded. 'Give your names to my sergeant and he'll see that his officers are told. But please don't go any further afield than your hotel in Montaz for now.'

I wondered idly whether I might also do well to take a room at the hotel. It would all depend how things went with my canine sleeping companion tonight. My only other experience of sharing the van with Oscar had not been auspicious, mainly due to the fact that he snored like a trooper and clearly believed all the floorspace belonged to him. Meanwhile, the inspector turned towards me.

'Signor Armstrong, I wonder if you'd be good enough to translate while I interview the two people who found the body? Maybe in there?' She indicated the tent and I nodded my consent before translating for the benefit of Bethany and her friend. They stood up hesitantly and the four of us walked across to the tent. In the meantime, other officers had arrived in a minivan and were donning disposable overalls and surgical gloves, ready for a detailed search of the crime scene. Around the campfire, there was just dazed silence.

5

WEDNESDAY AFTERNOON

Inside the tent, Inspector Costey asked the young couple to sit down and tell their story. I sat beside the inspector and acted as interpreter while the uniformed sergeant took a seat at another table and started writing on a lined pad. His companion remained at the door of the tent. After a short exchange of glances with Peter, Bethany spoke first.

'Peter and I went out last night at just before nine. We took the track up through the woods towards the observation post.'

'But surely it was dark by that time?' Inspector Costey interrupted her and I translated.

'The sun had set but it wasn't completely dark. We had torches and we know the track quite well now after walking it so often over the past few days. We followed it up to just before we reached the narrow path that goes off to the right, the one that leads up to the top of the hill, and it was there that we heard a roar and saw the flames off to the left of the track.'

'A roar, you say? Not an explosion?'

'Not really. It didn't go bang like a bomb or anything. It was more of a loud whoosh sound.' Bethany glanced over at her companion and he nodded in agreement.

'I thought it sounded kind of like a jet engine.' Although Bethany sounded British, Peter had an American accent.

'And you saw nobody?'

He shook his head. 'Not a soul.'

'And what did you do then?'

Bethany took up the tale again. 'We ran into the forest towards the flames for maybe about fifty metres or so and we found a fire raging furiously and starting to spread through the undergrowth. Another few minutes and it would have reached the lower branches of the trees and then God knows where it would have spread to.' She paused to take a long, calming breath. 'At first, we didn't realise there was anybody in the midst of the flames so we picked up fallen branches and started beating out the fire so that it wouldn't go any further. It was only as it died down that we got close enough to see that there was a body lying there in the middle of the embers.'

'Did you recognise it as your friend?'

I saw Bethany shudder. 'It was barely recognisable as anything. It was awful.' Her voice cracked and she reached for a hand-kerchief.

Her companion caught hold of her other hand and held it. 'It was grim but, like Julian said, Nick wasn't really a friend. He'd only arrived late on Monday and he wasn't exactly approachable.'

'What do you mean by that?'

'Most of his face was swathed in bandages and he kept himself to himself. He said he'd had an accident and had just come out of hospital. I don't know if it hurt him to speak, but he hardly said a word all day yesterday.' For a second or two, his expression lightened. 'To be honest, Beth and I started calling him The Mummy behind his back.' His smile disappeared. 'I feel sorry for laughing at him now.'

This was interesting. Not only had the man kept himself to himself but, by the sound of it, he had effectively been in disguise. Could this have been a deliberate ploy? If he had been trying to conceal his identity, it was presumably because there had been somebody here at the camp who might have been able to recognise him otherwise. Had he really been in hospital or had he chosen to use bandages and a story of an accident to remain anonymous and, if so, anonymous to whom and why?

Inspector Costey carried on with the interview. 'So if the body was unrecognisable, why did you assume it was Nick Green?'

Peter answered. 'We felt pretty sure it was him because of his walking poles. He had a pair of those ski stick things and they were lying beside the body, all warped and twisted from the heat of the fire. That and the fact that his car's still here.'

'His car?'

'He wasn't camping up here with us. He was staying at the hotel in the village down the hill and he drove up and back each day. It had to be him.'

'And where's his car now?'

'It's the black one out there, the Mercedes with Swiss plates. I presume he must have rented it.'

I relayed this information to the inspector and she and I exchanged glances. We both knew what this meant. If Green had rented the vehicle, he would have had to produce his driving licence so it should be possible to confirm his identity that way.

The inspector shot an order to the police officer at the entrance to the tent and he hurried off to check the vehicle while she returned her attention to the English couple. 'And you're sure you didn't see anybody else around? No noises in the trees? Footsteps, the sound of a car, anything?'

Bethany answered for both of them. 'I'm sorry, no.'

'And why did you decide to go for a walk in the dark?'

'We were going up to relieve Crispin and Geoffrey.'

'Relieve them?'

'We've all been taking it in turns to man an observation post up on top of Mont Saint Georges. That's the higher of the two little peaks above the camp. It's about twenty-five minutes on foot from here.'

'That would be for the purpose of looking for signs of extra-terrestrial life.'

'Yes. Julian's broken up the days into three-hour shifts. We were supposed to be on from nine to midnight. To be honest, we were running a bit late but we knew Geoff and Cris wouldn't mind. In fact, Nick was supposed to be up there with them from six, but they said he never showed.'

'And who took over from you at midnight?'

'I'm afraid with everything that happened last night, we came straight back to the camp with Crispin and Geoffrey and I don't think anybody else went up there until daylight.' Bethany paused. 'I think we all thought it was too dangerous – I certainly did – even though all the lights of the police and ambulance would almost certainly have frightened them off.'

'Them? You mean the killers?'

She didn't reply so the inspector tried again.

'Dangerous in what way?'

She exchanged another glance with Peter, who took over. 'We were worried the same thing might happen to us.'

'So you felt that you might be murdered?'

'Are you so certain it was murder?' Peter was looking unsure. 'To be honest, we don't think it was. Nick was probably just in the wrong place at the wrong time.'

'How so?'

'I believe he was killed by the exhaust blast of an alien craft. We've been seeing lights up in the sky every night and we believe the visitors must have landed.' Peter didn't raise his eyes from his hands and for a second, the inspector and I exchanged glances and I saw her raise a sceptical eyebrow.

'You believe the victim was killed by extra-terrestrials?'

'Yes, but I'm sure they didn't do it on purpose. Nick must have been too near when they took off and he got caught in the blast from the engines.'

I seriously doubted whether extra-terrestrial visitors would use the same means of propulsion as NASA, but I said nothing and waited for the inspector to continue. When she did, she avoided voicing any doubts about Peter's hypothesis, but I could almost feel the disbelief emanating from her all the same.

'And I understand you contacted the emergency services?'

'Sort of. Because none of us speak Italian, I left Bethany with the others and cycled down to the restaurant in Montaz. Luigi there speaks good English and I got him to make the call.'

'I see. Have you anything else to add? Anything that you think might help us in our investigations?'

The response of them both was to shake their heads although just for a second, I thought I spotted something on Bethany's face: fear maybe, just like I thought I'd seen on Julian's face.

Once the uniformed officer had finished taking down the statements, I read them back in English, and Bethany and Peter signed them. After that, the inspector thanked the couple and let them leave. Once they were outside, she looked across at me and lowered her voice to little more than a whisper. After all, we were separated from the others by only a thin wall of canvas and twenty metres of grass. All right, we were speaking in Italian and supposedly nobody in the group would understand, but we only had their word for that and so it was wise not to take any chances.

'What do you think of their story, Signor Armstrong?'

I was pleasantly surprised to have been asked. 'Cremated by a flying saucer? I've seen some strange things in my time but that would be a first for me. It strikes me as highly unlikely.'

'I agree, but I must admit they sounded convinced.'

'They certainly did, but I suppose they wouldn't be up here if they weren't converts to the UFO cause. From Peter's accent, he's American, so maybe he even came all the way over from the States especially for this event. The fact of the matter is that an exhaust blast doesn't explain the blow to the head, does it – assuming there were no rocks around that he could have hit by accident? I imagine we can rule out suicide as it's hard to set fire to yourself once you've just smashed your head in with a rock or whatever. By the way, the whoosh sound they claim to have heard is very much the noise petrol makes when it ignites.' I remembered the mistake I had made years ago of using petrol to relight a smouldering bonfire at home and the sound was imprinted in my memory – along with the singeing smell as I had lost part of my eyebrows. 'If we discard little green men, then there's not much left. In my experience, criminals set light to things to destroy the evidence. From what Bethany said, it sounds as if the fire did a very good job of concealing anything there might have been. Is there enough left of the body to make a post-mortem worth doing?'

She shook her head. 'I haven't seen the corpse yet but, according to the local police who were first on the scene last night, it was so badly burnt it was barely recognisable as human. I'm waiting for another call from the pathologist to tell me if he's able to give us anything more, but I'm not too hopeful. When we spoke earlier, he told me there was no way he could provide even a vague time of death so it's quite possible the victim was murdered earlier than nine and the body burnt later on. We need to establish the last time the victim was seen alive.' She glanced at her watch before looking up at me. 'I'd like to take a look at the crime scene next. I won't need your services as an interpreter up there, Signor Armstrong, so I'll go up with the rest of my team while you stay here.'

At that moment, the police officer from the door reappeared with his phone in his hand. 'It's a rental all right, Inspector. Swiss plates and there's a Hertz sticker on the windscreen. I've told the station to get hold of the company and ask them to send across a copy of the licence.'

'Thank you, Chanoux.' She turned to the sergeant. 'Right, Fournier, let's go up to the crime scene. When we get back, I want to get fingerprints and statements from everybody up here, detailing where they were yesterday between dawn and 10 p.m. And you'd better collect their passports. Nobody's going anywhere until we find out what this is all about.'

I nodded approvingly. Inspector Costey knew what she was doing. I just hoped she would be able to climb the hill in her condition – from the look of her, the baby could put in an appearance at any time. I pointed out of the door towards the campfire. 'I'll see if I can squeeze any more information out of the campers while you're away. Then if it's all right with you, I wouldn't mind taking a look at the crime scene myself once your officers have finished their search.'

'Of course.' She hesitated. 'And thank you for your help so far.' Her tone was definitely friendlier.

I glanced down at Oscar, who met my eye and gave me a satisfied look. Yes, it appeared that Inspector Costey was loosening up.

6

WEDNESDAY AFTERNOON

Back outside, Julian and his partner had returned to their campervan and the burly cameraman had also disappeared. Their places on the log by the fireside had been taken by another couple. These two were clutching steaming mugs of tea and looked tired. As Val plied me with yet more tea, she informed me that the new arrivals had been on UFO watch on the hilltop all morning and had just returned to be replaced by Libby and Alice. The others remained seated as before, most of them still visibly shocked by what had happened.

The couple that Libby and Alice had just replaced would certainly have stood out in an identity parade. The woman, Sybil, with her multicoloured jacket apparently made of bits of woollen blanket sewn together with a multitude of different colour threads and her unruly mass of hair, reminded me of the crazy cat lady in *The Simpsons*, while her partner, Wilfred, bore an uncanny resemblance to any number of depictions of Moses holding the Ten Commandments. He had a mass of white hair hanging down to his shoulders and one of the bushiest beards I had ever seen. He looked as though he hadn't used a razor for decades. I looked on in fascination as he lifted his mug to the area where his mouth presumably lay. It was like watching a conjuring trick: now you see it, now you don't. In fairness, however, he didn't spill it all over himself and these two both managed to give me a genuine-looking friendly greeting when Val introduced me to them.

'Hello, Dan. It's good to have a bit of new blood in the group.' Wilfred was probably well into his seventies although it was hard to tell beneath all that hair. Sybil, his wife, looked about ten years younger. 'I was just commenting to Sybil that the turnout this year has been a lot smaller than last.'

Sybil was quick to point out the difference. 'Yes, but last year was only just across the Channel in Brittany. I think the cost of the long journey to get here put a lot of people off.'

'So does that mean there are lots more people in the group? Julian said something about that.' I tried not to sound too interested.

'At the last count, the fellowship had a membership of almost three thousand.' Wilfred must have seen the surprise on my face. 'Not bad, eh?'

'Wow. And how do I join?'

'Julian's the moderator. Just give him your thirty pounds and he'll sign you up.'

'I see.' Three thousand members each paying thirty quid added up to a useful money-spinner for whoever was running the fellowship – presumably Julian. Of course, it could be he had high overheads. 'And what do I get for my membership fee?'

'You can access the monthly blog and get news of all recent encounters. We find it a most valuable source of information.'

It didn't sound as though there were any particularly high overheads after all. Presumably, no office or staff. Julian was onto a good thing, and not just as far as the sub was concerned, as Sibyl went on to demonstrate.

'And you can buy the official T-shirts and sweatshirts and hats and so on.'

To my surprise, she pulled open her coat of many colours to reveal a startling, lime-green T-shirt with the words *We Know the Truth* emblazoned across it in silver and the logo of the fellowship discreetly below it in white. It was the same poster I had seen on their Facebook page earlier. Add in the merchandising, and Julian was definitely doing well out of UFOs. And then there were his documentaries...

'I gather Julian has a TV company.' It wasn't a question, but it didn't seem to matter. Sybil appeared only too happy to reply.

'We've been watching all his programmes religiously, haven't we, Wilf? Julian goes all over the world in search of proof of alien life.'

'And has he found any?' I tried not to sound too sceptical as Wilfred replied.

'It's all around us. The world's littered with signs of extra-terrestrial activity from the Nazca Lines and elongated skulls in Peru to the Wedge of Aiud in Transylvania, from Aztec carvings to the remains of a UFO found in Antarctica.' Wilfred's eyes were gleaming as he reeled the names off. 'Every single continent has been visited, there's no doubt about that.'

'And has Julian found actual proof?' In case I sounded too much like a police officer, I hastily did my best to look excited. 'I do hope so.' I also made a mental note to google the Wedge of Aiud one of these days. As far as I knew, Transylvania was only famous for Dracula... or was that Frankenstein?

'Just watch his documentaries and you'll see.' I noted that Wilfred wasn't rushing to give me any examples of definite proof but I didn't press him any further on the subject.

'I certainly will. And they're called what exactly?'

'*We Know the Truth*.' Sybil indicated her chest. 'Just like the motto of the fellowship.' Then she brought the conversation onto more practical matters. 'It's such a shame about Nick's accident, isn't it?'

Evidently the news hadn't filtered through to Sybil yet, so I broke it to her gently and her response was shock and horror.

'Murder? But who on earth would want to murder him?'

'That's what the police are here to find out.' I could have added that I, too, wanted to work that out, but I kept silent. For now, I was just another ufologist and a helpful interpreter.

Any further reflection by me was interrupted by the feel of my dog's nose prodding my knee. He and I both knew what this meant by now so I finished my tea and stood up.

'Oscar wants a walk. Where would you suggest?'

'You could walk up to our observation post if you like. Alice and Libby are up there now.' Wilfred extended his arm upwards towards the rocky ridge running south to north a hundred metres or so vertically above the level of the camp. There were two distinct peaks partway along it and the higher of these was evidently where the ufologists had set up their base. Wilfred was looking less distraught at the news of the murder than his wife, but the shock on his face was still clear to see. 'Go up the track until you come to a spot where a narrower path leads off to the right. There are splodges of red and blue paint on the rocks put there by the Italian Alpine Club. You can't miss it. That's only a short way beyond the scene of last night's awful events.' His voice tailed off.

At that moment, I spotted Julian. He had emerged from his posh motorhome and he was striding over towards the fire, revealing yet more proof of his excellent hearing. 'I'm on my way up to check the observation post. I can show you the way if you like, Dan.' He looked around. 'Anybody else feel like a walk?' Getting no takers, he glanced across at me again. 'Looks like it's just you, me and your dog.'

I thanked him and we set off up the track, which wound its way up the increasingly steep slope towards the edge of the tree line. Glancing across at him, I could see that he kept himself in pretty good shape. Certainly, he wouldn't have had any trouble bashing the victim over the head. I also try to stay in good shape but I hoped I wasn't walking with a serial killer who might decide to try to clobber me over the head as well. Hopefully, this was not the case but I knew I had to be wary of everybody until I got to the bottom of exactly what had happened.

I spared another thought for the very pregnant inspector having to climb up unassisted and I hoped she would at least get a lift back down again. Fresh furrows in the soft terrain where vehicles had driven up and down last night and this morning had now been partially obscured by the feet of the platoon of police officers who had come up here to begin their search, unfortunately destroying any possible evidence left by the perpetrator or perpetrators in the process. As we walked, Julian and I chatted about generalities ranging from the weather to Italian cuisine before he brought the subject around to me.

'You said you live over here? What is it you do, if you don't mind me asking?'

'Not at all.' I was selective in my answer. I wasn't going to tell him the whole truth – yet. 'I'm a writer. My first book came out two months ago. It's a whodunnit set in Tuscany, which is where I live nowadays.' It seemed a good opportunity to learn a bit more about him so I turned the question back on him. 'What about you? Are you a full-time UFO watcher?'

He nodded. 'I suppose you could say that, among other things. In fact, I'm also a writer like yourself.' He glanced across at me and smiled. 'My book came out last year and I'm pleased to say that it's selling well.'

'Congratulations.' I decided not to tell him that my first book had been doing amazingly well and was now officially a bestseller. I had just sent off the second in the series to my publisher in London and I was waiting anxiously for her verdict. 'And is that fiction or non-fiction?'

'Definitely non-fiction. You may have heard of it; its title is *We Know the Truth*.'

Now why didn't it come as a surprise to me to learn that he had emblazoned the title of his book on the merchandise he sold? No doubt the book itself was also available on the website – for a price. Come to think of it, he had said that his TV company was called WKTTV. No prizes for guessing what the acronym stood for. As far as self-promotion and consistent branding were concerned, Julian was no slouch. 'And do you write about UFOs?'

He nodded. 'Contacts with extra-terrestrial beings, yes.'

'Alice told me you have actual first-hand experience of extra-terrestrials, what she called "the visitors". Is that really true?'

'It is.'

I waited expectantly for him to elaborate but he carried on walking in silence. I was just on the point of pressing him for a bit more information when we heard the unmistakable sound of a diesel engine coming down the track towards us. I called Oscar and we stepped off into the undergrowth as a dark-blue Land Rover with *Carabinieri* painted on the doors came bumping and lurching toward us. As it drew level with us, it stopped and a head appeared at the open window.

'There's a police search of a crime scene up ahead. Make sure you stay well clear of the restricted area and keep your dog under control.'

'Understood.'

As the vehicle set off again, I translated for Julian's benefit and he nodded, before replying in words that echoed what Bethany and Peter had said. 'I'm afraid with all the upheaval, we've almost certainly scared them off.'

'You mean the extra-terrestrials? How can you be sure they were here?'

'For the first three nights after we arrived here on Saturday, we've been seeing lights in the sky up above the tops of the hills coming down the main valley from the mountains. I've been trying to send them radio signals to tell them we're here and we want to meet them but, without knowing what frequency they're on, it's been like looking for a needle in a haystack.'

'Maybe they can't receive radio waves.'

He shook his head decisively. 'They certainly can. Scientists have been tracking unexplained radio waves emanating from deep space for decades now. It's just a matter of finding the right frequency.'

'You said you had proof of the existence of extra-terrestrials. Feel like letting me in on the secret?'

'It's no secret. It's all in my book. It happened in South America about ten years back. I was hiking on a remote track in the High Andes when I was approached by two beings. They appeared almost out of thin air and disappeared the same way. They must have had some kind of cloaking device for their craft, I suppose.'

'When you say "beings"...? What did they look like?' I almost asked if they were small and green but managed to restrain myself.

'They looked like you and me, with legs and arms, a bit smaller than us and they were wearing silvery spacesuits, just like our astronauts do on the moon.'

This sounded like a scene from the scaly things movie, but I suspended my disbelief for now. 'And did they talk to you?'

'Alas, no.'

'So you just stood there?'

'I folded my hands in the universal peace sign – you know, like Buddha – and they did the same in return.'

'And then...?'

'And then they were gone.'

'Leaving no trace, or do you have any proof of what you saw?'

'Of the beings, no, but I do have photos of the scorched earth left behind by their rocket engines. I can show you later on my laptop if you're interested.'

'Definitely.' This chimed with what Bethany and her boyfriend had said about the victim's burnt body, although I still doubted whether invisible alien craft would use the sort of fuels that would leave scorch marks. 'What did the landing site look like?'

'Like I say, the earth was scorched black. There was little or no vegetation up there at over four thousand metres to catch fire, but there were clear imprints of four triangular feet in the ground, presumably where the craft settled.'

At that moment, the track turned a corner and we saw that a cordon of police tape had been strung up on the left of the track to keep out intruders. Beyond it, a line of white-clad figures was engaged in a meticulous sweep of the surroundings while the blackened area in the middle of the zone was unmistakably where the fire had taken place. I spotted Inspector Costey right at the edge of the ashes, staring down, deep in thought. A uniformed policeman was standing by the track and he repeated the message we had received from the *Carabinieri* officer. In case we didn't fully understand, he added a few peremptory hand gestures that were a long way from the universal sign of peace.

7

WEDNESDAY AFTERNOON

We carried on up the track, with Oscar inspecting and marking just about every tree we came to, until we reached the edge of the tree line and emerged onto open mountainside. Patches of lush, green grass dotted with pink flowers were interspersed with outcrops of rock covered in lichen and moss, with tufts of heather pushing up here and there. Here we turned sharply to the right onto a narrow path marked with blobs of red and blue paint as Wilfred had said. This led up towards the highest point still some way above us. The path zigzagged up the ever-steeper gradient until we were having to scramble up the bare, rocky slope. I didn't envy the UFO enthusiasts making this journey in the dark. I certainly hoped that Inspector Costey wouldn't be expected to struggle up here in her condition. Even Oscar was panting by the time we got to the top. Certainly, Wilfred and Sybil were fitter than they looked if they had managed to get up here in one piece.

At the summit, we found a cairn with a thermos resting on it and two folding chairs alongside it. On them were the now familiar figures of Libby and Alice. Both had binoculars and there was a shiny, metallic, mirror-like sheet propped up against the cairn, presumably some sort of primitive communication device. Oscar wandered over to give it a sniff and I kept a close eye on him. Somehow, I doubted whether Labrador pee would add to its chances of opening communication channels with other worlds.

UFOs or no UFOs, the view all around was stunning. From up here, the vehicles down at the camp looked tiny, and the roofs of buildings down on the valley floor well over a thousand metres below that looked like Monopoly pieces. To the west, there was no mistaking the massif of the Mont Blanc living up to its name as the sun reflected dazzlingly off the brilliant white covering on what was the highest point in Europe. Over to my right, I once again saw that massive pinnacle of bare rock reaching into the sky at the head of the valley alongside an even bigger, but less barren, mountain. Presumably the one on the right was the Monte Rosa so that meant that the one on the left had to be the Cervino. I queried this with Julian and he explained why it looked familiar to me even if its name wasn't.

'The one on the right is the Monte Rosa. You can ski up there on the glacier all year round. The rocky one to the left is what the Italians call the Cervino. You and I probably know it better by its Swiss German name, the Matterhorn.' Seeing comprehension spread across my face, he continued. 'We normally see pictures of it from the Swiss side in Zermatt. It's the reason we're here.'

'You're here for a mountain?'

'We believe that the Matterhorn is used by extra-terrestrial visitors either as a navigation point or maybe it has some other, more important significance. Some people say it's magnetic or maybe it even contains a hidden base from which the visitors emerge to survey the Earth.' An expression of regret crossed his patrician features. 'Alas, nobody has been able to get proof of that hypothesis. Maybe this will be our chance.'

He left me to digest this information while he went over to the two ladies to consult the 'log' and talk about extra-terrestrial matters. I concentrated on matters closer to home. Apart from the muted voices behind me, the only noise was a distant tinkling of cowbells and I glimpsed a small herd of predominantly light-coloured cattle away to my right on the open pastures. I looked back down at the stick figures of police officers in the trees way below us as they combed the area, and I wondered if they would find anything. Assuming the fire *didn't* have an extra-terrestrial origin, the best they could hope for would be the rock or club used to crack the victim's skull or traces of an accelerant like petrol or maybe a few spent matches. An empty matchbox with fingerprints would be a welcome bonus but I wasn't holding my breath.

Just for a moment up here, in the warm sunlight of an early May afternoon, I allowed myself to question my scepticism about extra-terrestrials and visitors from outer space. I'm not a religious person and I have a deep-rooted trust in the ability of science to explain how life on earth developed. At the same time, up here, staring up at the almost cloudless arc of the sky above me, I knew that to assume that we are alone in the universe was hopelessly arrogant. After all, we are only little beings on an insignificant blue planet in among a multitude of other heavenly bodies, so incalculably numerous, they outnumber the grains of sand on a beach. Surely it was inevitable that there were other life forms out there, and it wasn't beyond the bounds of credibility that they did indeed visit Earth from time to time. Could it be that Julian really had met a couple of 'visitors'? Had the unfortunate Nick been killed not by a human hand but by some sort of interstellar spacecraft after all? As I had so often drummed into the officers under my command, one should always keep an open mind – however unlikely something might seem.

I turned back towards the UFO spotters with their folding chairs and their mugs of coffee and wondered what the 'visitors' might make of these visionaries ready to welcome them with open arms. Certainly, they wouldn't be able to fault the dress sense of these three or, indeed, their physical features. What they would make of me and my dog was another matter. Shaking off my doubts, I slipped back into my assumed role of UFO aficionado and went across to study the 'log' for myself.

I found that it was a simple exercise book whose pages had been divided up with pencil lines into four columns marked *Day, Time, Event* and *Observer*. The first column had been filled in scrupulously with dates since Saturday, presumably when they had first set up camp here, and the second and third columns held notifications of events on each of the first three nights. Initials in the right-hand column indicated who had made the sightings. The event entries were all between midnight and 1 a.m., although there was nothing for the previous night, no doubt because the watchers had abandoned their post after the death of the mystery man. The three entries all contained the same cryptic wording, *L/S-/Wh/C/5* followed by different initials in the *Observer* column. I glanced over at Julian.

'Translation, please.'

'We use a simple shorthand: L is for Lights, S minus means no sound, Wh is the colour, C means the lights were constant rather than blinking, and 5 is the number of minutes the object was visible.'

'So on three consecutive nights from Saturday to Monday, and maybe last night if people had been on watch, there have been unblinking, white lights in the sky with no sound and each event lasted around five minutes.' A thought occurred to me. 'Did Bethany and Peter tell you they heard a roar at around nine o'clock last night as the fire started, so shouldn't that be added to the log?'

Julian actually smiled. 'Yes, indeed. It certainly should.' He took the book from me, produced a pen from his pocket and wrote alongside the previous day's date: *2100/Fire/S+/ B&P.* 'I'd better double-check with them to find out how long the fire lasted.' As he handed the book back to Alice, he gave a little grunt of satisfaction. 'Excellent. That means we've had events four nights in a row. That's very unusual.'

I couldn't help adding, 'As is having one of your group carbonised by a UFO.'

The smile disappeared in a flash. 'Yes, of course. That was truly terrible but I'm sure they didn't mean him any harm. He just must have been in the wrong place at the wrong time.' He glanced across at Alice and Libby, who were staring at the sky, before turning his eyes back on me. For the first time, I realised how almost hypnotic they were: a most unusual green colour with an unsettling glint in the sunlight. 'They come in peace, you know. We're quite sure of that.'

The wrong place at the wrong time. This was the second time I'd heard this, so presumably it was the party line. As we had moved on to the subject of the murder victim, I thought I might try a couple of innocent-sounding questions. Whatever Julian and the others might think, in spite of my recent musings about the origin of the species, I felt convinced that the death of 'poor' Nick was going to turn out to be a terrestrial affair.

'Why do you think he was in that particular place at that time of night? It would have been sundown and pretty dark in the woods. Might he have got lost?' I already knew that he had been supposed to join the shift of the two nerdy men, Crispin and Geoffrey, but he hadn't put in an appearance. Had he been attacked en route to the top and, if so, by whom? 'Of course, maybe he wasn't on his own.'

For a second or two, Julian looked blank. 'Surely if he'd been with somebody, they would both have been caught in the blast.' He sounded unsure but I felt I could hear something else in his voice.

Did this mean he might have something to hide? This set me thinking. Up here was a pretty isolated place to choose for a night-time walk. Wasn't it more likely the victim had been with a companion and, if so, might not that same person be the one who had bashed him over the head and then set fire to the body? Trying not to sound too much like a detective, retired or not, I queried whether this might be a possibility.

'But if he wasn't alone, who was with him? Nobody from your group?'

Julian shook his head. 'No, not as far as I know. The thing is, Nick didn't really know any of us and we didn't know him. He was a bit of a loner, staying at the hotel and not really mixing with the others.' His voice was level once again. 'Besides, I'm sure if somebody had been with him, they would have spoken up. Apart from anything else, surely they would have raised the alarm.'

'Indeed.' I chose not to add the obvious deduction from this that if somebody had been with him and hadn't raised the alarm, the finger of suspicion of murder must surely point directly at that person. Doing my best to demonstrate only casual interest, I tried one more query.

'What sort of person was Nick?' Alice and Libby had trans-ferred their attention from the heavens to me now, so I threw out the question to all three of them.

They shook their heads in unison and, predictably, Julian answered for them. 'Like I said, none of us knew him. He turned up out of the blue the day before yesterday, just like you did today, and he was staying down at the hotel in the village rather than up here with us.'

I glanced at Alice and Libby. 'So was he staying at your hotel?'

Alice nodded. 'Yes. I assume that like us, he wasn't a great fan of caravanning.'

I gave her a grin. 'You sound like my girlfriend. That's why she didn't come with me.'

She managed to smile back at me. 'And Brian and Don are staying there too.'

These last two were new names to me. 'I don't think I've met Brian and Don. Were they here last night?'

Julian consulted the schedule on his phone. 'No, they were on watch yesterday afternoon and they're back on again at six tonight.'

'And did you know *them* before?'

Once again, he shook his head. 'No, they're first-timers as well.' Maybe noting my expression, he explained further. 'The thing is, we have literally thousands of members and I only know a handful of them by sight.'

'What about the rest of the group? Didn't you tell the inspector you knew a few of them before coming here?' I hoped I wasn't coming across as too inquisitive but, for now at least, they didn't appear suspicious.

'I met Sybil and Wilfred last year in France, and I know Isabel, of course, but this time, all the others are new faces to me.'

'Isabel's your wife?'

'My partner.'

I saw him make an effort to change the subject and I wondered if that was because he didn't want me to probe his relationship with Isabel. I remembered that proprietorial look on his face when I had been chatting to Libby and noticed that she was now pointedly staring in the opposite direction. I didn't have much time to ponder this as Julian turned the conversation back to me.

'What about you, Dan? Are you a member of the fellowship?'

'No, not yet. I must do something about that.'

'I've got everything in my mobile home. You can drop in any time and maybe buy yourself a copy of my book while you're at it.

I'd be happy to sign it for you.' Upset or not, he hadn't lost his business acumen.

'Of course.'

I stayed up there for a while, reflecting on what I'd learnt since arriving at the camp. Somehow, I had assumed the ufologists would be a tight-knit community of old hands who regularly met up, but clearly, in this instance, this was not the case. The next question was how many of the others had known each other before coming here, but that would best be left to the inspector to find out. I had already asked a load of questions and I didn't want to appear too inquisitive so I just nodded, leant against the cairn, and admired the view. One thing was for sure: I had no intention of handing over thirty quid to Julian to help fund his designer shirts.

8

WEDNESDAY LATE AFTERNOON

I went back down to the camp again around mid-afternoon and it was half past six before the inspector and I finished the interviews, and statements had been taken down and signed by each of the ufologists. Inside my head, I felt pretty sure that the killer had to be one of the group. Of course, it was possible that the murderer had been some random person out walking in the hills in the dark or somebody who had sneaked up here to commit murder, but it seemed highly unlikely. When Alice, the last of the ufologists to be interviewed, had walked out of the tent, I soon discovered that Inspector Costey was thinking along the exact same lines.

'We'll send off a list of the names to the UK in the hope that your former colleagues over there can turn up anything interesting about any of them, including the victim, but we're still waiting for Hertz to send us his details. But unless it turns out that the man had a murky enough past to make somebody decide to send a hitman all the way out here to kill him, my feeling is that our murderer has got to be one of the people we've just interviewed.' She was speaking in a low voice so as not to be heard outside the walls of the tent. 'I'd appreciate a bit of your time tomorrow if you can spare it. I'd like your help to go through the information we receive from the UK when it comes in.'

'I'd be happy to help.'

At that moment, Sergeant Fournier appeared at the door of the tent. He had news.

'We've just heard back from Hertz. They've sent over a copy of the victim's driving licence and it turns out he was using an alias up here.' He handed his phone across to the inspector, who consulted it and then handed it to me.

'Mean anything to you, Dan?'

I was so keen to see the licence, I almost missed the fact that Inspector Costey had actually called me by my first name for the first time and had even used the familiar form of the pronoun 'you'. It appeared that I had been accepted. I studied the licence on the screen and saw that Nick Green was in fact Richard Brown, age fifty-three, with his address given as one of the posher roads in Notting Hill, London. I studied the photo closely. He was another good-looking, well-groomed man, but his face meant nothing to me. I handed the phone back to Inspector Costey and she voiced the question that was on my own lips.

'Why the alias?'

I nodded. 'And why the disguise?'

'Green and Brown – aren't those two colours in English?' She gave me a little smile. 'I had to do English at school as a second language after French so I'm afraid not very much of it sank in.'

'You're right about the colours. Yes, not the most sophisticated of aliases. Come to think of it, Richard is often abbreviated to Rick in English, so he wasn't really trying terribly hard when he chose Nick, was he? If he was some sort of spy, he was either new to the job or not very bright, so I think it's safe to conclude that Richard

Brown wasn't an espionage professional. Do you think he might have been connected in some way with somebody up here, Inspector?'

She looked up. 'Call me Carmela.' I felt Oscar nudge my leg. He was probably just keen to remind me that dinner time was coming up, but I often wonder how much he understands. Certainly, her response was confirmation that I really had been accepted as part of the investigation. 'Yes, I think it's almost certain that there was somebody here who would have known him.'

I scratched Oscar's ears. 'And maybe that somebody recognised him and killed him, but why?'

'What motive could somebody here have had to murder a fifty-three-year-old Englishman halfway up an Italian mountain?' Carmela Costey was looking as puzzled as I was feeling. 'By the way, the pathologist called and he confirms that the severity of the blow to the head would have killed him outright, so the fire was presumably so as to destroy any evidence.'

I was equally puzzled. 'What evidence? It's not as if there were bullets or knives involved. Why start a fire that's bound to attract the emergency services?' This had been nagging at me all afternoon, as had the sheer brutality of setting fire to a body. Whoever had done this had either been a cold-hearted killer or a very sick person – or both. 'If the protagonist had simply dumped the body in the bushes, that would almost certainly have given him or her days to get away before anybody stumbled on it. And, if they'd come with a shovel, they could have buried the body out here and who knows when it would have been discovered, if ever? It makes little sense.'

'The pathologist's trying to retrieve any clues from inside the body in case there might be traces of drugs or bodily fluids but, given the severity of the fire, he's struggling. He says he's going to need dental records to confirm the man's identity; it's that bad. Of course, it could simply be that the killer didn't want people to know he'd stolen the man's wallet and ID. I'll get a check done on Richard Brown's credit cards and passport just in case somebody's using his identity.'

'Good idea. That could be the explanation for the fire but I'm still not so sure somebody would commit murder just for a passport and a credit card or two.'

'Nor me. What makes robbery even less likely is that the pathologist found the remains of a Rolex watch on the man's wrist. Still, we need to check all possibilities. Until we get the results of the enquiries from London, we're in the dark.'

'By the way, I couldn't take notes during the interviews today but it seemed to me that most of them had alibis. Who was the last person to see the victim alive and at what time?'

'The tea lady, Valerie Gough – however you pronounce it – and her daughter said they had tea with him between five and five-thirty yesterday. He then set off for his shift on observation duty and, as we know, he never arrived up there. According to my records, they were the last to see him alive.'

'So theoretically, the murder could have taken place any time after that, quite possibly *immediately* after that. What if the killer waylaid him on his way up to the top? Anybody who looked at the observation schedule would have known he was meant to be going up there then. The pathologist said he had no way of knowing when the victim was murdered, didn't he? From the testimony of Peter and Bethany, we know the body was set alight at between nine and a quarter past nine, but he might already have been dead for hours. We could well be looking for a killer who smashed the victim's head in at, say, sixish, and then came back to hide his or her tracks at nine by setting fire to the body, although it's a barbaric thing to do – but then, so is bashing somebody's head in. Alternatively, maybe the murder was committed by one person, and then another person entirely came along and set fire to the body as much as three hours later.' I glanced up at Sergeant Fournier. 'Do we know where everybody was from, say, five onwards?'

The sergeant, who had been standing in silence, checked his notebook. 'Most of them have alibis of a sort, but some of them were in their individual campervans and so the alibis are generally provided by their partners, which doesn't prove much. Both people could have been complicit in the murder. Two have no alibis and these are Elizabeth Winter and the cameraman, Wayne O'Connell. O'Connell claims to have been out in the woods taking background footage for the documentary he's filming, and Elizabeth Winter says she went for a run from four to five and then went back to her hotel. She's a health fanatic apparently and she runs every day. Nobody can corroborate these stories.'

I had a thought. 'You could get him to show you what he filmed. I imagine that will be timecoded so you can probably work out where he was and when. As for Libby (that's a contraction of Elizabeth, and everybody here calls her Libby) Winter, she looks as though she takes a lot of exercise, so her story could well be true. Besides, would she have had the strength to club somebody to death?'

Fournier continued. 'The only ones with reasonably safe alibis are the tea-making mother and daughter and Sybil and Wilfred Smith, the elderly couple. The four of them claim to have spent most of the late afternoon and evening sitting around the campfire. Apparently, they didn't know each other before coming here so, if that's true, there's no reason why they would lie to protect the others.'

'Anybody else?' The inspector was flicking through her own notes. 'What about the woman we've just interviewed?'

'She has a reasonable alibi.' Fournier glanced down at his notebook. 'Alice Turner. She says she drove down to Montaz at four-thirty and went for a walk around the village before returning to the Albergo Italia at five, where she went to her room and stayed there until six, when she went and had a drink in the bar. She then had dinner between eight and nine-thirty. She claims the staff there will be able to confirm that.'

I remembered her telling us that and I was secretly pleased to hear it. Alice looked far too nice to be a murder suspect. No sooner had the thought occurred to me than I gave myself a mental ticking-off. How many times had I told my men not to let themselves be swayed by appearances? Some of the most notorious killers we'd caught when I was at the Met had had the faces of angels.

I turned the other names over in my head. 'So that leaves us with five pairs of suspects whose alibis have been provided by themselves: Julian and his partner, Isabel, Geoffrey and Crispin, the nerdy boys, Bethany and Peter, who found the body, my friend from Scotland Yard's sister, Sandra, and her friend Maggie, and don't let us forget Brian and Don, the weirdos.' I used the Italian slang word '*stramboide*', which I had recently learnt, and I was rather proud of it.

I saw the inspector and the sergeant smile and at the same time felt a heavy paw land on my foot and Oscar gave me another nudge. Clearly, he was fed up and wanted a walk. I glanced down at him. 'Two minutes and we'll go, okay?' Returning my attention to the inspector, I summed up the situation as I saw it. 'So pretty much any of those ten plus the cameraman and Libby the jogger could have done it. That's virtually all of them. Did your search of the crime scene come up with any clues? I haven't had a chance to take a look for myself, but I will, I promise.'

'Yes, I've been meaning to tell you.' The inspector was looking pleased with herself. 'We found two items of considerable interest: an empty plastic bottle lying in the undergrowth near the track and smelling strongly of petrol. I've sent the bottle off for finger-printing but I don't hold out too much hope. Surely the killer would have worn gloves but you never know, we might get lucky. But, more importantly, we found the murder weapon: a large lump of rock with clear bloodstains on it. It was lying in a clump of brambles only about ten metres from the body where the murderer must have thrown it. It's too rough for prints but we've sent it off anyway. Otherwise nothing, not even a spent match.'

'The rock and empty bottle are about as much as we could hope for. One thing's for sure: they definitely prove that the murder wasn't as a result of alien activity.'

Carmela shot me a little grin. 'The ufologists will be disappointed when they find out, but let's keep them in suspense for a little bit longer. By the way, what did you think of the two guys who're staying at the hotel? What was it you called them, "the weirdos"?'

'They're certainly weird. Even for how I imagine UFO fanatics to be, these guys are off the scale.'

Brian and Don had driven up to the camp from the hotel at five that afternoon and had been interviewed then. They had both clearly been itching to start their observation shift, even though it wasn't scheduled until six. I could see that they took their UFO hunting very seriously indeed. They had expressed shock at the news of Richard Brown's murder although it hadn't appeared to affect them that much, even though they had been staying in the same hotel. Like the others, they claimed they hadn't known him before coming to Italy and had hardly seen him while they had been here. In fairness, he had only arrived the night before his death. The other reason why he maybe hadn't mingled with them so much was the appearance of these two. I had a feeling most normal human beings would have reacted the same way. The description of them as weird was putting it mildly.

Both claimed to be from London, both were in their forties and both were male, but that was where the normality ended. Seen from afar, Don might have looked pretty normal, but close up he was anything but. His completely shaved head had been tattooed with obscure symbols and hieroglyphics and he looked like a living representation of the Rosetta Stone. His neck was similarly decorated and, for all I knew, the tattoos might well have continued on down his body. I had no desire to find out.

His companion, Brian, had a gold ring in his nose, more earrings than a pirate and a pair of matching pigtails, unusually front and back. The one made from hair from his head ran down his spine and reached almost to his waist while the bizarre pigtail made by plaiting his beard probably risked a soaking every time he picked up a glass. In case this wasn't weird enough, both were dressed in identical shiny silver jumpsuits, no doubt intended to look familiar to any aliens – particularly of the B-movie kind – but this only made the two of them look more like seventies DJs. I couldn't help wondering whether their choice of attire might have been inspired by the description of the alien beings in Julian's book.

I did my best to translate one of my dad's favourite sayings into Italian. 'There's nowt so queer as folk' came out as 'There's nothing so strange as people'. It didn't sound so good but the police officers smiled so maybe it worked in Italian as well. I carried on with summing up. 'Those two didn't shed too many tears over Richard Brown's death, but I suppose they didn't know him well enough to care that much. Most of the group looked shocked to different degrees but, of all of them, I thought Julian, the leader, and his partner, Isabel, looked the most suspicious. I have a feeling he knows more than he's letting on. If you've finished with me for now, I'll go and take a closer look at the crime scene and then I'll try to get Sandra Wilson on her own and find out what she meant when she told her brother she thought there might be something fishy going on.'

9

WEDNESDAY EARLY EVENING

The opportunity to talk to Paul's sister came sooner than I had hoped. I was just on my way up the track to check out the crime scene for myself when I met Sandra running down towards me.

'Something wrong?'

She came to a halt and shook her head. 'No, it's just that I've remembered that I left my phone on charge in the van and I'm going to need it if we see anything tonight. The rota's all out of kilter today so Brian and Don are on observation duty now and Maggie and I are on our way up to join them, even if it's not officially our turn. She's desperate to see some signs of alien life.' She glanced around nervously. 'You're Paul's old boss, aren't you? I met you once.'

I nodded. 'Dan Armstrong and Oscar at your service.'

To my surprise, she flung her arms around me and hugged me. Oscar, not to be left out, stood up on his hind legs and joined in the group hug.

'Thank you so much for coming, Inspector Armstrong. I've been really scared.'

I glanced around but there was nobody else to be seen. 'Just call me Dan. I'm no longer on the force and nobody here knows my real identity apart from the police. Have you got two minutes? We need to talk.'

She nodded so I asked her to tell me all she knew, which turned out to be precious little.

'Ever since Nick Green appeared, the atmosphere here has been weird.'

That word again. Considering the appearance of some of her fellow ufologists, it wasn't just the atmosphere that was weird, but I left that unsaid and asked her to explain.

She spread her hands out helplessly. 'I don't know. It's hard to describe.'

I did my best to help her. 'Was there anybody in particular who was behaving weirdly? What about Julian and Isabel? How were they?'

'To be honest, they've been behaving strangely ever since we got here. I would have expected them to be happy to be here and interested in the chance of seeing some signs of extra-terrestrial life, but they've been getting ever more taciturn. Maybe things aren't going too well between them or maybe it was the arrival of Nick, I don't know.'

'Julian told me nobody knew who the new guy was. Are you saying you think maybe he or his partner recognised him?'

'I really don't know, but it wouldn't surprise me.'

'Was anybody else behaving strangely?'

'Wayne the cameraman has always been a bit uncommunicative, a bit distant, but at least he wasn't unpleasant. Since the arrival of Nick, I've never seen him smile. And the same could be said about Libby.'

'So do you think either of these people recognised Nick?'

'Maybe... it's hard to say. It could be they didn't actually recognise him, but it was just his bizarre appearance. It was as if the arrival of this strange man swathed in bandages cast a cloud over the whole group. And, of course, after he was found dead, it's been awful.' She looked around nervously again. 'If he really was murdered, I'm terrified I might be next.'

'Why you?'

'Well, not me specially, just any one of us. What if there's a crazy killer among us? He might kill again, anybody, just like that.' She glanced at her watch. 'Can we continue this later? I really need to get my phone and then hurry back up to join Maggie.'

I made a quick decision. 'Go and get your phone and then I'll walk back up with you. There's something I need you to do for me from now on: please try not to go anywhere on your own and only go out with somebody you know and trust. Will you promise me that?'

'Yes, of course, but does that mean you think there really might be a crazy, homicidal maniac among us?' There was fear in her voice. 'I mean, there are some strange people here.'

'I honestly don't know. I think it's highly unlikely but it's wise not to take any chances.' She was still looking scared so I offered a bit of encouragement. 'Don't worry, I'll be watching your back. I know that's what your brother wants. The more I think about it, none of the group should be walking about on their own. I think I'll mention it to Julian.'

She gave me a hint of a grin. 'What about you? You're on your own.'

'On my own? Not on your life. I've got my faithful guard dog to protect me.' The fact that my faithful guard dog was stretched out on the ground at her feet, grunting happily to himself while she rubbed his tummy with the toe of her boot, didn't exactly support my assertion, but she appeared to accept it and we set off down the track. Just before we reached the open ground, I stopped and waited in the trees while she went back to her campervan and collected her phone. Val, the tea lady, and her daughter, Millie, were still at the campfire along with Sybil the crazy cat lady and her Old Testament prophet lookalike husband. Everybody else had retired either to their vans or into the tent. The sun was still hot enough to make me glad I could wait in the shade. It wasn't even mid-May but the sun had real heat in it. It occurred to me that I should probably put on sunscreen since we were so high up.

On the way back up to the hilltop, we met Geoffrey and Crispin coming down the track towards us and they informed us with regret in their voices that, although they had also been up at the observation point for several hours, there had been nothing to report as far as extra-terrestrial activity was concerned. Geoffrey's T-shirt now looked as though he had added coffee to the spilt beans on it. Pretty soon, he would have a full English breakfast on there.

Sandra and I carried on uphill with Oscar happily looking for sticks for me to throw for him to retrieve. A woodpecker could be heard hard at work not far away from us in the trees and the only other sound was the gentle sighing of the breeze in the branches. From time to time, the trees around us thinned and allowed us to look back over the camp and down into the valley far below. In the distance on the other side of the valley were the distant snow-capped mountains of the Mont Blanc massif. It really was delightful. Under other circumstances, it would have been a very pleasant walk. Pity about the killer on the loose.

Up at the cairn, Don and Brian in their shiny suits were deep in conversation, poring over a laptop screen, so Sandra and I had the chance to take her friend Maggie to one side without arousing suspicion. I told her what I was doing here and I asked her to keep my identity secret. As far as all the others were concerned, I was just another ufologist. I also repeated my advice to the two of them to avoid going off on their own. She looked relieved to see me and I could tell that she, like Sandra, was scared.

Leaving them with the silver-clad duo, I walked back down to the crime scene and looked around. The police had removed the tape before leaving and, apart from the burnt area, there was nothing to show that this had been the scene of violent death less than twenty-four hours earlier. There was no point looking for footprints as the multitude of boots had destroyed all traces there might have been of the killer. There was, however, one thing that caught my eye – or, rather, four things.

Around the scorched earth where the victim had been burnt were four triangular impressions in the soft ground. Interestingly and suspiciously, they hadn't been trampled on by any of the investigating officers and were still clearly distinguishable. They formed the four corners of a square roughly four metres across and they immediately made me think of Julian's story of his alien encounter in the High Andes. If I didn't already know that Richard Brown had been bludgeoned to death with a club or a rock, I might even have felt tempted to buy into the notion that these marks were the proof that an alien spacecraft had indeed landed here. I took photos of the marks to pass on to the inspector and took a good look around for any clues as to their origin – which I felt sure had nothing to do with alien beings.

My discovery in the bushes ten minutes later of a piece of an old wooden fencepost confirmed my suspicions. There was fresh earth stuck to one end of it, presumably indicating that it had been used to create the triangular shapes in the damp ground, and this further pointed to their terrestrial origin. Somebody had waited until the police had finished searching the crime scene and then had come up here subsequently and made those marks. I picked up the piece of timber with care and took it back to the camp, where I hid it in a bush before emerging into sight of the others. I would collect it later and hand it over to the inspector, who would no doubt send it for fingerprint analysis. I felt pretty sure that I wasn't going to be surprised when the identity of the mystery mark-maker was revealed.

Back at the campfire, I was on the receiving end of yet another mug of tea from Val and a proposition, or at least an invitation. The tea was very welcome and the invitation came from Alice.

'Dan, as you and I are both on our own, I was wondering, how would you feel about joining me for dinner at the hotel tonight? Libby's tied up doing some work thing with Julian. Did you know he's been interviewing some of us for a programme that he's making about what he's calling "the incontrovertible proof that the Matterhorn hypothesis is a real thing"?'

After what Julian had told me, I now knew what this was, but I feigned ignorance. 'What's that?'

'There's been a lot of talk about the Matterhorn being used by extra-terrestrials to navigate or as a base, and Julian's determined to be the one to provide proof.' She shot me what looked suspiciously like a sceptical glance. 'That would do his reputation no end of good in the field of UFOs.'

'For the "interviews", he actually primes people with what he wants them to say. It's hardly very professional. Anyway, if you feel like having dinner at the hotel with me, I'd be grateful, otherwise I might end up having to eat with the Pirates of the Caribbean. They're staying at the Albergo Italia as well.' She had lowered her voice although Don and Brian with their tattoos, rings and pigtails were still up at the observation post and nowhere to be seen.

'That's a good idea, I'd be happy to. I only had cheese on toast for lunch so I'm definitely up for a good meal tonight. Do you think it'll be all right to bring Oscar?'

'I'm sure it'll be fine. The German couple on the next table to me last night had a pair of sausage dogs with them. What time would suit you? It's almost eight now, so say in half an hour?'

We agreed on half past eight and after she had headed off in her little silver hire car, my conscience started telling me I should call Anna. All right, I was merely having a meal with a new acquaintance, but I didn't want either of the women to misconstrue what was happening. I finished my tea, thanked Val and walked away from the campfire. When I was sufficiently far away not to be overheard, I pulled out my phone and made the call. Anna answered almost immediately.

'Ciao, caro. Come stai?'

I answered in English, which she spoke better than I did Italian, after having lived and worked in the UK for years before returning to her native Tuscany. 'Hi, Anna. Having a lovely time. Wish you were here.'

'You've got Oscar to look after you, you don't need me – especially if you still plan on sleeping in your car.'

'We're staying in the van tonight but there's a hotel not far down the hill so I might check in there tomorrow night, even if it's just for the sake of a hot shower.'

We chatted and she told me about things at the university and I told her about the investigation. When I mentioned that Inspector Costey was a woman, a suspicious note entered her voice. 'Just because she speaks your language – that's the language of policing, not English – don't you go getting ideas.'

I assured her that nothing was further from my thoughts – adding, just for good measure, that the inspector looked as if she was about to give birth at any moment. However, in view of Anna's suspicion reaction about Carmela, I decided that now was not the time to reveal that I was about to have dinner with another woman and we parted, as always, on good terms. I glanced down at Oscar and gave him a wink. 'You're a very good dog but I wish I were spending the night with Anna, not you.'

He looked up and wagged his tail. He probably would have preferred to be spending the night with Anna as well.

I was just wondering if I might have time to call into the café down the road for a cold beer before my dinner date when my phone started ringing. I checked the caller ID and saw it was my daughter, Tricia.

'Hi, sweetheart, how's things?'

'Hi, Dad. All good with me, thanks. You okay? You doing anything special?'

Either she called me or I called her once a week. Since her mother had divorced me, Tricia and I had been getting even closer, in spite of the distance between Tuscany and Birmingham, where she worked as a solicitor. She and her fiancé, Shaun, had come over and spent a week with me at Christmas and it had turned out to be a lot of fun.

'I've come north and I'm camping in the Alps for a couple of days. If you really want to know, I'm doing a bit of UFO spotting.' I kept my voice low although there was nobody around.

'You're doing what?'

I explained that I was doing Paul a favour by keeping an eye on his sister and told her what was going on, but Tricia's response wasn't what I was expecting.

'UFOs, did you say? Does that mean you're involved with the murder of that actor chap? Rick somebody? Brownley... Browning. Yes, Rick Browning.'

'Did you say "actor"?' This was news. Nobody had so much as hinted at that. 'How do you know that?'

'It's on the TV this evening and I expect it'll be in the papers tomorrow with a headline like: *Soap Star Killed by Aliens*. Not that he really was a star, at least not nowadays, and you bet your life he wasn't killed by extraterrestrials. He used to play a minor character in *Eastenders* but they killed him off and I doubt any people remember him now. They said on the TV that he's made a bit of a name for himself doing documentaries since then, but I didn't realise who he was until I saw his photo on the news.'

'Blimey...' How had the media got onto the story so fast? The name on his driving licence was Brown so presumably he called himself Browning as a stage name. More concerning was the possibility of the camp now being assaulted by journalists although if, as Tricia had said, he was no longer that well known, maybe the London-based tabloids wouldn't bother with the expense of sending anybody.

'So, Dad, is that why you're there? Playing at being a detective as usual? Well, good luck with it. I hope you find your killer.' Her voice became more serious. 'Just you be careful. I wouldn't want anything to happen to you, especially if you haven't got Anna up there with you to look after you.'

'Don't worry, I've got Oscar. He'll protect me.'

No sooner had she rung off than I called Carmela Costey and broke the news to her that the story had reached the UK media. I heard her groan.

'That's all I need. I've just heard back from the pathologist that he hasn't been able to find anything of interest in the corpse apart from the fact that his nose was broken, probably when he fell forward after being struck on the head. Dental records are on the way – hopefully, we'll get them some time tomorrow – so we can make a conclusive positive ID. There's no sign of a wallet or any documents, but the pathologist said the blaze was so intense that probably means nothing.'

I also mentioned the freshly made marks in the ground around the UFO 'landing site', and it didn't surprise me to find that we both had the same idea as to who the culprit might be. She promised to take the piece of plank for fingerprint analysis the next day but we both agreed that the identity of the mark-maker and the murderer weren't necessarily going to turn out to be the same. She confirmed what I had assumed, namely that the marks had not been there when she and her officers had done their search and so must have been made long after the murder had taken place.

Finally, I queried if there was any way we could fend off a possible assault from the tabloids. 'Is there any way we can prevent journalists from getting up here if the story takes off? Or would it be better to get the ufologists to pack up and go somewhere else where you can keep an eye on them but where the press can't reach them?'

'Let's see how much interest his death generates before we worry too much. Maybe if he wasn't that famous, it'll all die down, but I'll leave the roadblock in place and tell the officers on duty to continue keeping people in as well as keeping people out.'

10

WEDNESDAY EVENING

I drove down to the restaurant at eight-thirty.

On the way, I called Paul at Scotland Yard to tell him that his sister was alive and well and that I'd been accepted as part of the investigative team. It soon turned out that he had seen the same media reports as Tricia about the death of Richard Brown aka Rick Browning aka Nick Green. He said he would make a few discreet enquiries to see if he could find out anything about Brown that might have made him a target. I told him Carmela Costey had sent a list of names of the ufologists to London for any helpful background and he promised to check with the records department handling this in case he could help them unearth anything useful to add to their report. That way, we should have all bases covered. We both agreed that it sounded very much as though one of the ufologists must have spilled the beans to the press and I spent the rest of the five-minute drive down to Montaz wondering who it might have been – most probably Julian in the search for publicity for his TV programmes, his money-making fellowship and associated merchandise.

There was no sign of life along the road until I reached the village, apart from a lone fox who slunk out of the undergrowth and slipped across the road as we approached. The village was a sweet little place that had probably been not much more than a farming settlement until tourism here in the valley had taken off in a big way. It really was a remote location. As a place for a murder, it wasn't bad, although the fact that the only access or escape was by a single mountain road wouldn't have made it first choice for a professional killer. This made it ever more likely that Brown's killer was one of the people up at the camp. The car park in front of the hotel was already full so I left the van behind Alice's silver Fiat at the side of the building and walked around to the main entrance.

The restaurant occupied most of the ground floor of the hotel and both Oscar and I flared our nostrils as we walked in. Something smelt very good indeed. Alice was sitting over in the far corner, alongside a healthy-looking banana palm in a huge, terracotta pot. She looked very smart and I felt decidedly scruffy in my jeans and T-shirt – albeit a clean one – and without having had the benefit of a shower. As she bent down to pet Oscar, I got my apologies in fast.

'Hi, Alice. Sorry if I'm letting the side down but my van's a bit short of mod cons.' I decided not to tell her that I had taken a comfort break behind a convenient clump of conifers at the side of the road on the way here. 'What's the hotel like? I think I might book a room here tomorrow for the sake of a hot shower – as long as they'll take Oscar.'

She was still looking zonked and the bottle of red wine in front of her was already half empty, but she managed to produce a smile and waved me into the seat opposite her while Oscar subsided onto the floor between us with a thud and a heartfelt sigh. 'The hotel's pretty good and my room's clean and comfortable – can't ask for more than that. I'm on the ground floor and I even have my own little piece of garden. You look fine, Dan. It makes a change to see somebody up here wearing a plain T-shirt for a change, rather than one plastered with superheroes or *We Know the Truth*.' I couldn't miss the scepticism in her tone when referring to Julian's book. Maybe my initial impression that she wasn't as committed to the cause as some of the others was correct.

We chatted a bit about the area and I studied the menu while waiting for the waiter to come and take our order. Predictably, up here in the mountains, the dishes were hefty and highly calorific – which suited me after a fairly wearing day. Alice chose a simple mixed salad as a starter and then one of the local specialities: *bistecca alla valdostana*. She explained that she had discovered this the previous night and that it was a thin steak coated in breadcrumbs and fried with a slice of ham and a big chunk of melted cheese on top. She told me that it made a cheeseburger look like dogfood in comparison – although I had no doubt Oscar would have been happy with either. I immediately decided to have the same but I felt I needed something more substantial than salad as a starter so I decided on *crespelle alla valdostana*. The wine in her glass was disappearing rapidly so I ordered a bottle of the house red, which turned out to be Barbera from just down the valley in Piedmont.

Just to prove that I had a healthy respect for hygiene in spite of my dishevelled state, I excused myself and left Oscar with her while I went off to wash my hands. I was on my way back when my phone rang. It was Paul again.

'Hi, Dan. Bingo! It looks like we now know how the UK media got hold of the story so fast. One of the ufologists is a journalist, working for the *Mirror*. Her name's Alice Turner. Ring any bells with you?'

'It certainly does and, coincidentally, I'm about to have dinner with her. I imagine that might explain why she's staying at the hotel. She must be on expenses. I wonder what brought her here

in the first place. I get the feeling she isn't a 100 per cent committed
UFO fanatic so maybe she's here trying to get a story, debunking
the whole "visitors from outer space" thing. Suddenly finding
herself with a murder to report must have been the icing on the
cake. I'll see what I can get out of her and I'll let you know. Thanks
again for passing that on.'

I returned to the table feeling glad Paul's message had got to
me before tonight's conversation developed. I've never trusted
journalists and, apart from a few like my good friend Jess in
London who had managed to get me a full-page article in *The
Sunday Times* colour supplement that had kickstarted my new
career as a novelist, I've generally tried to steer clear of them. In
consequence, I was much more on my guard when we resumed
our conversation.

I did my best not to give anything away and decided to get her
to tell me about herself and, to my surprise, it appeared that that
was exactly what she wanted to do. She waited until the waiter had
brought her 'simple' salad – which was anything but simple with
quail's eggs, smoked duck breast and local cheeses mixed in with
three different types of lettuce – before she made a start.

'Dan, do you have a number for the police inspector?' She took
another swig of wine and it looked to me as though she was in
need of a bit of Dutch courage. Why? I wondered.

I hesitated for a moment. I certainly did have Carmela's
number but I didn't want to give Alice the impression that the two
of us were friends so I opted for caution.

'I know how to get hold of her. She's either at the police station
at Cervinia or at the *questura* in Aosta – that's the main police
station for the Valle d'Aosta. Why do you ask?'

Just then, my *crespelle* arrived and I felt movement at my feet,
followed by a heavy nose landing on my lap, nostrils twitching.
Oscar wasn't wrong. They smelt wonderful. I had had these tasty

folded pancakes filled with ham and cheese back in Tuscany, and the Valle d'Aosta variety were positively stuffed with cheese, no doubt from some of the cows I had seen on my way here this morning. I bought Oscar off with a chunk of crusty bread and busied myself with my food so as not to look too keen to hear what Alice had to say.

'I need to talk to her.' She sounded hesitant. 'You see, I didn't tell her everything when we spoke this afternoon.'

This was promising but I still acted as if the *crespelle* interested me more than what she had to say. 'Mmh, this stuff's good. What is it you want to tell her?'

'The thing is, when she asked me if I knew the victim before coming here, I said no, but that was a bit disingenuous.'

I sighed to myself. Why was it journalists and politicians could never bring themselves to use the word dishonest? I didn't comment other than to give another appreciative murmur about my latest mouthful of food while I let her say her piece.

'I mean, it's true that I'd never *met* him before, but I knew who he was. In fact, I was sent over here to follow him.'

'Sent? Who by?' I took a mouthful of Barbera and waited for her to explain.

'I'm a journalist. I work for the *Mirror* and we've been doing a series on celebs who get cosmetic surgery. We got word that Rick Browning – that's his stage name – was in a clinic in Montreux having a few nips and tucks, so I was sent over to check him out. When I discovered that he was a UFO fanatic and he was coming up here afterwards, I had to hastily develop an interest in all this nonsense.' She caught my eye. 'I'm sorry, that's unfair. I'm sure you truly believe all that stuff. I shouldn't mock other people's beliefs.'

'That's okay.' I wasn't going to reveal that I shared her sceptical opinion of UFOs and I pleaded ignorance of the victim in the hope of learning a bit more about him. 'I'm afraid I don't think I know an actor called Richard or Rick Browning.'

'He used to be reasonably well known in the UK soap-opera world, but never a really big star and certainly not famous internationally. The interesting thing is that he now hosts a series of programmes on TV about, guess what?' She didn't give me time to supply the answer. 'That's right, he works for a company that specialises in making programmes about the unexplained, starting with whether aliens walk among us.'

I shot her a grin. 'I'm seriously suspicious about your friends the Pirates of the Caribbean and their silver spacesuits.'

She smiled back. 'You and me both. Anyway, he works for a TV company called CosmosLink and they specialise in that sort of thing. I was sent over here with strict instructions not to reveal what I was doing and I had to get my editor's permission before I could say anything to the inspector.'

'I'm sure she'll understand.' My mind was racing. If Rick Browning represented a rival TV production company, had he come here to spy? And, if so, had he been recognised and killed? 'Tell me something – how effective was his disguise? Even if *I* didn't know him, surely some of the others would have done?'

'Not necessarily. To be honest, he hadn't done anything of note for probably as much as ten years. I doubt if anybody younger than me would be likely to recognise him, although I'm sure Julian and Isabel would have known him if they'd been able to see his face.' She stopped and I saw her rethink what she'd been saying. 'Come to think of it, I suppose he would have been quite well known to any of the ufologists who watched his programmes.'

'So, given that almost everybody up here is a committed ufologist, any one of them might have recognised him. The elderly couple, Wilfred and Sybil, told me they watch Julian's programmes religiously, so it's very likely they would have watched these others as well.'

'I suppose you're right, but the thing is that he'd just come from the clinic and much of his face was covered in dressings – and I don't just mean a few sticking plasters. I wouldn't mind betting that he turned on the charm with some friendly nurse in Montreux and got her to add a few layers of bandages so as to hide as much of his face as possible. You'd be surprised what a difference it made. I barely recognised him and I knew who he was.'

'How did you find out he was coming up here?'

She smiled. 'I found myself a friendly nurse of my own who – in return for a handful of Swiss francs – told me he'd been boasting about what a big TV star he was and how he was off to a UFO meet in the Aosta Valley. A quick online search and I found out that the only place hitting the UFO headlines around here at the moment was this one. I set off early on Monday morning and lay in wait for him back down the valley before Valtournenche. There are loads of hotels in the valley and I had no idea which he would choose. I waited a couple of hours before I spotted his black Mercedes come past and then all I had to do was follow him up here, wait until he'd checked into the hotel, and then I did the same.' She caught my eye. 'This is my job. It's what I do. They don't call it investigative journalism for nothing.'

This was interesting. If Brown really had been recognised as a rival and murdered because of it, then the finger of suspicion pointed well and truly in one direction only, but could I see Julian as a murderer?

'But why would anybody want to *kill* Brown?' I allowed myself to sound a bit more interested without sounding too much like a detective. 'I can't see how his presence at the camp could have annoyed anybody but Julian and maybe Isabel, but surely murder would have been totally over the top as a reaction to finding a spy in the camp?'

'I know what you mean. I've been trying to get my head around that as well. As far as I could tell, nobody up at the camp realised who he was or, if they did, they weren't letting on. My feeling is that Julian and Isabel *did* recognise him but didn't acknowledge the fact. I suppose it's possible that he was killed by somebody completely different for another reason entirely, but...' She hesitated for a moment. 'If I had to lay a bet, it would be on one of those two although I agree that it seems extreme. Maybe there was some other reason why they wanted him dead.'

There didn't seem to be a lot more Alice could add to the investigation without me getting too intrusive with my questions so I just pointed at her still almost untouched salad. 'Eat up. I've almost finished my *crespelle*. I can find the number of the *questura* easily enough and I'll give them a call in the morning and tell the inspector what you said. If she wants to speak to you further, I'll let you know. For all I know, she might be coming back to the camp in the morning anyway.' A thought occurred to me. 'Does this mean you'll be going home to London tomorrow?'

She shook her head. 'No, seeing as the police told us all to stay put until the investigations are over, I can't leave. Besides, my editor wants me to send him regular updates on how it's all going.'

I groaned inwardly. All I could do was to be gracious in defeat. 'You never know, by the time you leave, you might have seen visitors from an alien world.'

'Some hopes... Just one thing, Dan: please could you keep my identity a secret? As far as the guys up at the camp are concerned, I'm just here for the UFOs, even if I secretly think it's a load of baloney.'

So that made two of us, but I didn't let on. 'I promise, if you'll do something for me.'

'Of course.'

'Could you somehow manage not to give away to your readers exactly where we are? Apart from anything else, if you do, your competitors will probably be all over the area like locusts and any chance Julian and the rest of us might have of getting closer to the visitors from space would be lost forever.' It sounded a bit flimsy but she appeared to swallow it.

'It's a deal. To be honest, I was thinking of doing that anyway. Like you say, why give the opposition any useful information while I've got my hands on a scoop?'

'Out of curiosity, what sort of guy was Richard, Rick Brown?'

'Let's say nobody could possibly accuse him of having a lack of self-worth.' She caught my eye for a second or two and I read true disgust on her face. 'He thought he was God's gift.'

'Well, actors do have a reputation for being a bit egotistical.'

'A *bit*? The guy was almost twenty years older than me and just out of hospital, looking like something out of a horror movie, but when he first saw me on Monday night, he immediately started chatting me up – and I'm not just talking friendly chit-chat.' Her tone was as sour as her expression. 'Like I say, I'd never actually met him before but I knew he had a reputation for being a woman-iser, and he came across as a lecherous old git.' She took a mouthful of wine to remove the memory. 'He wouldn't leave me alone. Apparently, a night in bed with him would have been the experience of a lifetime for me.' She shot me a bitter smile. 'I'm sure it would have been, but not for the reasons he thought.'

'It would have made a good scoop for you, though.' I softened my words with a smile but she gave a pretty convincing shudder.

'Just because I work for the tabloids, that doesn't mean I'm totally unscrupulous. There's a limit to what I'm prepared to do to get a story.'

'I'm delighted to hear it.'

It was an enjoyable evening and the food was very good. As we ate, we chatted and under the influence of the wine, she began to visibly relax. I glanced around the room and began to notice a marked similarity between the predominantly dark photos adorning the walls. While waiting for my *bistecca alla valdostana,* I got up and walked across to study some of them more closely and it became clear that these grainy prints purported to be photos of UFOs. To be honest, most were little more than lights in the sky or just pinpricks in a featureless backdrop, but each bore a label listing meticulously where and when the photo had been taken. It came as no surprise to see that all claimed to have been taken on or near the hill where the ufologists had set up their observation post, Mont Saint Georges. As for dates, they appeared to range back over the past three years.

As I was standing studying them closely, I heard a silky voice at my ear.

'Are you interested in extra-terrestrial life?'

I turned to see that the voice belonged to a dark-haired Italian in his forties or fifties and as he was speaking reasonable English, I answered in English.

'That's right. I'm fascinated by the whole idea. Are you here for the same reason?'

He smiled. 'I live here – although I *am* fascinated by the thought of extra-terrestrial life.' He held out his hand towards me. 'Luigi Arnad. I'm the owner of the Albergo Italia.'

'Dan Armstrong.' We shook hands and I gave him a quick appraisal. He was playing the part of the affable restaurateur to perfection but my old copper's sixth sense told me that there was something insincere about him and I filed him away in my head as potentially untrustworthy. Still, I complimented him on having a fine restaurant and an excellent chef and his smile broadened.

'Thank you so much. We do our best. My grandfather set up

this hotel just after the war and my father took it on after him. Sadly, he passed away three years ago and I've been running it ever since.'

'Well, you seem to be doing very well. I see the restaurant's almost full tonight.'

He nodded. 'We've been almost fully booked since Easter and we've been lucky enough to keep fairly busy all year.'

I indicated the photos. 'Do many of your guests come for the UFOs?'

'A considerable number. The mountains around here have developed something of a reputation.'

And having a reputation like that was no doubt very useful in keeping occupancy high all year round in an out-of-the-way place like this. Ungenerously, I found myself wondering whether this was sheer chance or whether an ambitious hotelier might have found it helpful to propagate the myth. Might he somehow be responsible for the lights in the sky? All's fair in love, war and business.

11

WEDNESDAY NIGHT

After the excellent and very filling *bistecca*, I went out to the reception desk and asked whether they would have a room for me and my dog for the next night or maybe a bit longer. The young lady on duty assured me that they had space and that Oscar was welcome 'as long as he doesn't climb on the bed', so I told her I'd like to make a booking for one night, maybe two or three. I was walking back to the table for my very self-indulgent dessert of profiteroles when I remembered that I'd have to present my passport to her the next day and it occurred to me that the hotel might still be holding Richard Brown's passport or, at the very least, a copy of it. Italian hotels, unlike their French counterparts, always ask for proof of ID and sometimes hold onto the documents until the guests leave – a very easy way of ensuring that guests don't sneak off without paying their bills. I decided I had better query whether Carmela Costey had got her people to check that. Although we now knew Brown's real name, there might be clues in there as to why he had been killed. For example, a North Korean or Iranian visa would be bound to muddy the waters.

At the end of the meal, Alice accompanied me out into the square and surprised me with a suggestion.

'If you want a shower, my room's just upstairs.'

It was just as well we were outside in the dark, otherwise I was sure she would have spotted the uncertainty on my face. I told myself that this was merely a very kind and practical offer of help to a friend who was currently squatting in a VW van. Alternatively, it might have been more than that, and three things occurred to me simultaneously. First, she was theoretically still to be considered as a murder suspect – however unlikely this appeared. Second, she was many years younger than me and could surely do better than a retired copper who was going grey, and lastly and most importantly, I was already in a solid and meaningful relationship with Anna. I thanked Alice but declined her kind offer – whatever its actual nature – thanked her for her company and went off around the corner of the building to the van.

I set off up the road to the camp and on the way, I stopped in a convenient parking spot and called Inspector Costey to ask whether her people were checking with the hotel for Brown's passport, and to pass on what first Paul and then Alice had told me about her real purpose in being here. I heard the inspector give a frustrated snort.

'Well, at least we now know how the media got hold of the story. Thanks a lot, Dan. As for the passport, I plan on calling into the hotel tomorrow morning. I ran out of time today.'

I was still harbouring a vague sensation of guilt after Alice's probably quite innocent proposal about the shower, so I called Anna just to check in with her again and mention my dinner companion. When she answered, I found myself struggling for the right words. Whether it was feminine intuition or something else, her immediate reaction when she heard my voice was to check that

I was all right and then to put me on the spot. 'Dan, you sound like a naughty schoolboy. What have you been up to?'

'I haven't been up to anything… honest.'

She could probably hear my blushes over the phone. 'Come on, tell the truth. What's the matter?'

Sheepishly, I told her I had been having dinner with a younger woman who had offered me the use of her shower and I had just wanted to check in to assure her that I had refused and she need have no concerns about me going up to Alice's room for any reason. To my surprise, and relief, she burst out laughing.

'Dan, *amore mio*, you are such an idiot. I know you and I trust you, but it's very sweet of you to call. So tell me, what was she like, this younger woman? Was she beautiful?'

I gave her a brief description of Alice, making sure to emphasise that she was in no way more attractive than Anna herself, and told her about the discovery that Alice was a journalist. When I went on to tell her what I'd found out about the victim, she came up with a very sensible suggestion.

'Would you like me to ask Zia Menca about this guy? You know she's deeply into all these stories of the unexplained and I wouldn't be at all surprised if she's heard of him and his TV programmes. Maybe she can provide a bit of background or a bit of gossip. Come to think of it, give me the details of this Julian character and I'll ask her about him and his company as well.'

It was just after eleven when I got back to the camp and parked in my original spot. The fire had burnt down to little more than glowing embers but there were still two people sitting by it. Before taking Oscar for his evening walk, I went across to say hello and found Sybil in her coat of many colours with her husband alongside her.

'Hello, Dan. Have you been out for dinner? Want a *digestivo*?' Wilfred produced a bottle from down at his feet and offered it to me. One look at the label told me it was grappa. Now, some grappa can be good, some even very good but, in my limited experience, an awful lot of grappa is more suitable for fire-lighting or paint-stripping than human consumption. I wasn't familiar with the label on this one so I decided discretion was the better part of valour.

'Thanks for the offer, but I've had more than enough to drink tonight already.' Although I hadn't drunk anything like as much as my dinner companion. 'I've just had dinner at the hotel in Montaz and it was a very good meal. Have you tried it?'

'No, but we were all supposed to be going there for dinner some time this week or next, weren't we?' Wilfred glanced over at Sybil for confirmation.

'That's what Julian said, but I wonder if it'll still go ahead after everything that's happened.' Sybil glanced at her watch. 'He and Isabel went up to the observation post a short while ago. We'll be there ourselves in a few minutes. The rota's a bit funny today but we think we might be supposed to be relieving whoever's up there on duty. Besides, this is the time the aliens appear and it's unbelievably thrilling to see the lights.' She was positively bubbling with excitement but, I told myself, this was precisely why they had come all this way. To Sybil and Wilfred and most of the others, seeing a few lights in the sky was the equivalent of a gold hunter finding a nugget as big as your fist.

The supposed sightings of lights in the sky had been between eleven and one so I decided to wander up the hill with them, not least as in my adopted persona of ufologist, it would be the natural thing to do. I felt confident I wasn't going to witness any visitors from another world but, even so, there was a little part of me that was fascinated to see what all the fuss was about.

The temperature was noticeably lower than earlier in the evening so I picked up a fleece from the car and a few minutes later, we set off up the track. By now, my eyes had become accustomed to the darkness and we didn't need to use torches, which was just as well, considering that all I had with me was the torch app on my phone. When we reached the top, I saw that, not only were Julian and Isabel here, but also Geoffrey and Crispin, as well as Brian and Don, whom I was mentally referring to in Alice's terms as the Pirates of the Caribbean. Wayne, the cameraman, had set up his tripod and camera, and Julian was doing a piece to camera. I stopped and listened with growing fascination.

'Here we are high on an Alpine peak, waiting for incontrovertible proof that we're not alone in the universe.' He stopped, allowing several seconds of dramatic silence before suddenly reaching up and pointing towards the heavens. 'Watch with us as we await the arrival of alien beings: beings that have already killed a fellow human.' Now his expression darkened and he leant forward towards the camera. 'Alas, one of our band of brothers of the fellowship was burnt to death only a few days ago. Might we be next?'

After another dramatic pause, he straightened up and ran his hand across his throat. 'Cut, Wayne. That's a wrap.'

As Wayne redirected the camera towards the sky, I reflected on what I'd just heard. Clearly, Julian was embracing recent events to his own advantage and trying to create an air of mystery and apprehension. Considering that a man had been murdered and then cremated in such a macabre way, it struck me as distasteful and it did little to endear me to Julian or his cause. Whether it made him capable of murder, however, remained to be seen.

Meanwhile, everybody had returned to their places and all eyes were on the heavens. Clearly, from the number of observers, I wasn't the only one to have worked out that prime time for UFO spotting on Mont Saint Georges was about to start.

I settled down on an outcrop of rock beside the cairn and

waited. The temperature was even lower up here and it was cool enough for me to be grateful for my fleece. There wasn't a cloud in the sky and, although the moon hadn't yet risen, the stars cast enough light for me to be able to make out the shapes of the other figures up there with me and the outline of the mountains on the horizon all around. The pyramid-shape of the Matterhorn was unmistakable and I found myself wondering if there could be anything in Julian's thesis of it being a point of interest for alien travellers.

All eyes were trained on the sky and there was an expectant air in the group. I leant back and relaxed while Oscar stretched out at my feet and was soon snoring, untroubled by the prospect of an encounter with extra-terrestrial beings. To be honest, after a big meal, I had to struggle to keep my own eyelids open.

We stayed like that for almost an hour until around half past midnight, when there was a sudden flurry of activity among my companions. They were all equipped with binoculars, and the Pirates of the Caribbean shared a telescope on a stand, and all were pointed to the north, towards the Matterhorn. Although I had a pair of binoculars back in the van, I had stupidly forgotten to bring them up here with me tonight and I resolved to remember them next time I came up. I heard Julian snap an instruction to the cameraman and a chorus of hoarse whispers indicated that they had spotted something. I strained my eyes to see what it might be.

Following the direction of the big telescope, I gradually began to make out a distant light in the sky, coming ever nearer. To the naked eye, there was little more to be seen than a light: maybe an aircraft of some sort. I listened hard, struggling to hear the noise of an engine, but all I could hear were occasional whispers and even a gasp or two from my companions. Still at high altitude, the light – which might have actually been three or four lights in a cluster but without binoculars, it was impossible to tell – passed over our heads before suddenly zigzagging sharply to the right and disappearing without trace. I looked across at Julian, who was standing stock-still, staring upwards in mute fascination, the starlight illuminating an expression of wonder on his face.

I cleared my throat to attract his attention. 'Was that what I think it was?'

He lowered his binoculars and glanced at me. I distinctly saw his catlike eyes gleaming in the starlight. 'That's four times – five if a craft really did land last night. That's remarkable. And each time, the objects appear from the north – that's the direction of the Matterhorn – and then disappear southwards. It appears that we're on a regular route.' I heard him take a deep, satisfied breath. 'I feel privileged to be here, don't you, Dan?'

'Absolutely.' What else could I say, although I was still far from convinced that what we had seen had an extra-terrestrial origin. Even so, I had to admit grudgingly that I was looking forward to coming back up here the following night with my binoculars.

12

THURSDAY EARLY MORNING

I had a reasonable night's sleep, all things considered. The seats of my van folded down to make a flat area extending to the back door but, of course, this meant that I had to share the space with Oscar. He thought this was great fun and the first ten minutes were a struggle to make him stay in his bed rather than try to climb into my sleeping bag with me. Finally, he appeared to get the message and settled down, but when I woke up early next morning, it was to find myself squeezed up against the side of the van with the dog's heavy head resting on my chest while he basked in the remaining space, eschewing his now empty bed.

Muttering dire imprecations, I climbed out into the cool morning air and took him for a walk, following a broad arc downhill from the camp for a change so as to check out the wider area. Although my suspicions remained firmly that our killer would turn out to be a member of the UFO group, it seemed sensible to see if any other people were in the area, either living in the wilds or just camping out. Here in the trees, it was remarkably quiet. Even the sound of the cowbells had disappeared and I could hear remarkably few birds. Maybe up here at two thousand metres or so was too high for them –

but I'm no ornithologist. About the only noise was the crunching of dry twigs and leaves under Oscar's paws as he foraged for sticks and pine cones. The vegetation here was a mixture of deciduous and evergreen trees interspersed with open areas of scrub or straggly grass and we walked for almost twenty minutes, down in the direction of the village, before seeing any serious signs of human activity.

What we did see were a couple of red squirrels in the trees above us and the silence was immediately shattered as Oscar erupted into a fit of belligerent barking as he tried, unsuccessfully, to climb the trees towards them. The squirrels' reaction to this was one of haughty disdain, and Oscar finally admitted defeat and followed me down the track. The other less welcome animal I came across a bit further down was a snake. I only spotted its tail as it slid hastily off into the undergrowth and I wasn't able to identify it, but I had a feeling there might well be poisonous vipers up here in the Alps. The last thing I wanted was for my canine buddy, or me, to get bitten.

The first sign of civilisation came as I was walking through a particularly thick clump of fir trees. I began to hear the sound of an engine and came out onto a gravel track, on the other side of which was a sloping orchard with a funny little tractor making its way between the rows of trees, harrowing up the weeds. Even though it was narrower than a normal tractor, there wasn't much room for it to squeeze between the rows and I was impressed at the expertise of the driver. I gave him a wave and received a lazy salute in return. Looking to my right along the track, I spotted buildings in the distance and decided to take a closer look.

It soon emerged that these had to be Il Convento, the café and farm shop I had seen indicated on my way up the road. Three or four cars were parked outside a long stone building, opposite which was the very welcome sight of tables underneath a solid-looking wooden pergola, roofed with bamboo to provide shade. A couple of ramblers in full mountain gear were having breakfast at one table and a wonderful smell of coffee filled the air. I decided to follow their example and a glance down at the Labrador told me he would be happy to join me.

As the air was still chilly, I took a seat in the direct sunlight and made sure I was a little bit away from the other table in case Oscar might decide to go begging for food. A minute later, a man emerged from the main house and came across to take my order.

'Good morning, what can I get you?' He was a very tall, power-fully built, black man and although his Italian wasn't bad, it clearly wasn't his native language.

'I'd love some breakfast, please. A cappuccino, some bread or a croissant and maybe some fruit juice. What've you got?'

'I can press a couple of oranges for you if you like, or we have last season's apple juice.' He was doing a pretty good job of speaking slightly hesitant Italian, but it occurred to me that he might be more comfortable in English.

'Is that made from apples on your own trees?' I asked the ques-tion in English and saw a little smile appear on his face as he answered in the same language.

'I picked them myself last September, sir.' He pointed over towards the orchard through which Oscar and I had come. 'We store them in the convent's cellars where they keep well and the juice is very tasty.'

'Then I'll have a glass of that, thank you, and I don't suppose there's a drop of water for the dog, is there?'

'Of course, sir. Leave it to me.' His English was really excellent and I wondered where he was from. Over the past years, a growing flow of migrants from sub-Saharan Africa have been arriving in Italy and many of them are more fluent in English or French than

Italian. Living up here was probably providing quite a change in temperature, compared to where he had come from.

The breakfast, with home-baked bread and home-made straw-berry jam, was excellent and Oscar evidently appreciated the bowl of water that the waiter brought out for him and the crusts off my bread. The man stayed and chatted for a minute or so and I learnt that his name was Conrad and he came from the state of Kaduna in north-west Nigeria. I told him my name was Dan and I was British and I saw his eyes light up.

'I have friends in England. They tell me it's a wonderful coun-try, full of kind, tolerant people.'

I decided not to disabuse him. Over my years in the Metropolitan police, I had come up against numerous exceptions to this description – some of them members of the police force itself – but, on reflection, maybe it wasn't so bad after all.

'England's good but, if you want my opinion, I really like Italy. I'm living here full-time now and I love it.' And I did.

When Oscar and I had quenched our thirst, I went across to the stone building to pay. The name of the place translated as The Convent and I studied it with interest. The long, low, stone construction was bereft of decoration or any of the sort of grand architectural splendour of many other ecclesiastical buildings here in Italy and I wondered what its history was. I got the chance to find out when I went inside. Sitting at the cash desk was an elderly priest who beckoned me in as I stuck my head through the fly curtain.

'It's all right. You can bring the dog in with you. I love all animals and we only get a health inspection once in a blue moon.'

I smiled at his choice of vocabulary. He used the Italian expres-sion whose literal translation is, 'Every time a pope dies'. Considering the dog collar and black robe he was wearing, this indicated a nice sense of humour. Inside, there was a small selection of produce on sale and, from the look of it, most of it had been produced here on the spot. One of the things I love about Italy is the way you can still find good local food and I picked up a jar of apricot jam and a loaf of what looked like home-made bread and resolved to come back in the van later on and stock up. As I paid, I queried the history of the convent.

'Convent is actually a misnomer.' The priest sounded pleased to have been asked. 'It started life in the thirteenth century as a monastery, a little abbey, founded by an offshoot of the Cistercians.'

I had come across the Cistercians numerous times in my medieval research and I was able to show him that I knew who they were and that their ethos had been one of poverty and hard work in the fields. He nodded in agreement.

'Exactly. And that's exactly the spirit we're trying to nurture in our guests. By "guests", I don't mean our clients like yourself; I mean the men who work here.'

'Like Conrad.'

'Exactly. We've been operating for five years now and we provide board and lodging for recently arrived migrants and we help in getting them work and residence permits. In return, they help with running the farm and they learn useful skills at the same time.' He smiled. 'In actual fact, many of them come from a farming background and I've been learning a lot from them in return.'

'That sounds like a very worthwhile service you're providing. How many guests do you have here at the moment?'

'Eighteen. We were twenty, but two left recently for permanent jobs down in Turin. Conrad will probably be the next to go. His papers are all going through and hopefully, he should get his permits in the next few days or weeks.'

'I wish you, and them, lots of luck. I'll be back later on to do some shopping.'

'That's good to hear. Are you living locally?'

'Only until the weekend. I've been up at the camp – you know, with the ufologists.'

'Really? But there's been a terrible tragedy up there, hasn't there?'

'I'm afraid so. All very sad.'

'People are saying it was murder. That's not really true, is it?'

'It looks like it, but there's no cause for concern. The police are on it.'

'Do they know who did it?'

'I really couldn't say. Anyway, see you later.'

As we were walking back up through the woods again, I got a call from Inspector Costey.

'*Ciao*, Dan. Sleep well?'

'Sleep? No time for that, Carmela; I was up all night watching unidentified flying objects.'

I heard her laugh. 'Yes, and I'm Father Christmas. Listen, I've had the report back from London on the victim. It's in English and I think I've got the gist of it but I'd like you to go through it with me, if you don't mind. I'm on my way up to Montaz now. Could we meet up, somewhere private?'

I glanced back over my shoulder. The roof of the convent was still visible through the trees so I suggested we could meet there and turned back.

When I got back to the convent, the police car had just arrived and Officer Chanoux was standing by while his boss heaved herself none too easily out of the passenger seat. She waved when she saw me, and Oscar trotted over and gave them both a warm greeting. The three of us sat down at the same table where I had just had my breakfast. After we had ordered cappuccinos for

Chanoux and me, and a decaf for her, she laid a folder on the table in front of us and I made a start with the translation.

'The report confirms what I heard last night: Richard Brown, stage name Rick Browning, actor, fifty-three, residing in Notting Hill, London. Recently treated at a private clinic in Montreux, Switzerland. No details given, but the clinic specialises in cosmetic surgery. After studying acting, he got a series of jobs, the best known of which was a part in a long-running British soap opera. After that ended, he moved more into presenting and worked on several documentaries for Sky for a while before getting his current position with CosmosLink TV five years ago. He was front man for a series of TV programmes about UFOs and all that stuff as well as producing regular podcasts. He developed quite a following among like-minded people, although he was only on the fringe of mainstream TV. Married twice but divorced by his most recent wife four years ago. Infidelity on his part cited in both cases.'

The inspector nodded. 'That ties in with what your dinner companion last night told you about him being a bit of a womaniser.'

'Anything else? Any previous convictions?'

I checked the file. 'Nothing on record apart from a couple of speeding offences. No, he looks clean from that point of view.'

'Any connection between him and Julian Goodfellow or the Fellowship of the Silver Orb?'

'Again, nothing on record, but it's clear he was a believer in all that stuff – or at least somebody who was prepared to pretend he did for the sake of his career – so I'd be surprised if they didn't at least know *of* each other, if not know each other more closely.'

'Any connections with any of the other ufologists here?'

'They're still looking into it, but I think you need to take Julian Goodfellow to one side and get him to tell you all he knows about

Brown.' She nodded in agreement and I carried on. 'If he discovered the victim's real identity, he has to be our number one suspect for now, although I'm not sure I see him as a killer. Alice Turner told me she didn't think anybody else up at the camp had recognised Brown apart from maybe Julian and Isabel, but of course it's possible one of the others did and kept it quiet.' I remembered something. 'Did your people get a chance to check the video footage shot by the cameraman on Tuesday? Anything of interest?'

She smiled. 'Nothing to firmly establish his locations – mainly just lots of trees and sky – but an interesting sequence when the camera follows Elizabeth Winter as she runs down the track towards the police roadblock.'

'Why interesting?'

'Because most of it is in extreme close-up of the woman's bottom in spandex shorts.'

'Umm, Wayne and Libby, eh? Or at least Wayne had an interest in her, even if it wasn't reciprocated.'

At that moment, Carmela's phone started ringing. It was a brief conversation that consisted of her listening intently and uttering a few murmurs before ending with the words, 'I'll come right back.' She dropped the phone and looked across the table at me. 'That was my office. UK police have sent over the background information on the rest of the ufologists. Of course, it's all in English as well. My people are printing it off now and I wonder if you could come and talk me through what it says.'

'Of course. Where do I come to?'

'The *questura* in Aosta. My intention was to sit down and question Julian Goodfellow and his partner this morning, but this is more urgent. I'll pop up to the camp now just to check that there have been no developments overnight and then I'll stop off at the Albergo Italia to see if they have Brown's passport, or at least a copy, but then I'll head right back to Aosta. It's a forty-five minute drive. Can I give you a lift? Chanoux will give you a lift back again.'

'Thanks, but it's probably best if I take my own vehicle, partly because of Oscar but also so that the campers don't think I'm too closely linked to your investigation. Besides, that way, I can take a look around Aosta after we've finished. I've driven past often enough but I've never stopped off in the town.' A thought occurred to me. 'While you're at the hotel, you might like to ask if they have any CCTV footage for Tuesday. After all, four potential suspects are staying there and it would be useful to double-check the stories they've given us.'

Carmela gave me a smile. 'Thanks, *Commissario* Armstrong, I rather think the Metropolitan police lost a good detective when you retired. It's a pleasure working with you.'

I grinned back at her. 'The feeling's mutual.'

Oscar and I hurried back up through the trees and made it in just over fifteen minutes. If I had been a little chilly before, I was boiling now. It had been a steep climb. Before setting off in the van, I checked with Val to see if I could bring her some more milk or anything else. I didn't tell her where I was going so as to maintain for a bit longer the fiction that I wasn't involved with the investigation. She gave me a big smile.

'A few pints of milk and some eggs would be lovely, thank you, Dan.'

13

THURSDAY MORNING

The drive to Aosta entailed going back down all the hairpin bends to Valtournenche and then retracing my steps to the main valley where I turned right in the direction of the Mont Blanc tunnel and Switzerland and drove the remaining twenty kilometres on the motorway. In fact, the trip took me almost an hour, but of course I didn't have a flashing blue light on the top of my vehicle. The main valley was noticeably wider than the one I had just come down and this allowed me to see just how absolutely massive the mountains on either side really were. They rose thousands of metres above me and the tops of many were still covered in snow, even now in the month of May. The lower slopes were dotted with farmhouses and herds of cattle, whose milk was no doubt destined to become the region's famous Fontina cheese. If it hadn't been for the never-ending stream of heavy goods vehicles with registration plates from everywhere from Sweden to Turkey and beyond, it would have been a charming drive.

The way into Aosta was a long, straight road lined with garages, supermarkets, agricultural suppliers, ski shops and stores selling local cheese and wine. I made a note of the food shops and resolved to call in on my way back to stock up with supplies for Val and for myself to add to the home produce I intended to buy from Il Convento. A glance in the mirror at a big, black face staring hopefully at me reminded me that another big bag of dog food would be a good idea as well.

The *questura*, the main police station for the Valle d'Aosta, was a modern block on a wide road with easy parking, which made a pleasant change compared to the parking chaos around the Florence *questura* where Virgilio worked. I gave my name to the officer on the front desk and less than a minute later, Officer Chanoux came running down the stairs and accompanied me and Oscar up to the second floor. Here, I was on familiar-looking territory. I could have been back at Scotland Yard. Offices led off a central corridor and I could hear the murmur of voices, phones ringing, the hum of printers and other electronic equipment, and there was a smell of coffee in the air. On our way to Carmela's office, Chanoux stopped by a door marked *Commissario Pierre Gressan*, and glanced across at me.

'The *Commissario* wanted to say hello.'

He knocked and a voice from inside told us to enter. Chanoux ushered me in and stationed himself just outside in the corridor.

Commissario Gressan was probably a few years older than me, maybe in his early sixties. His short-cropped hair was snowy white, but he still looked active and fit. He jumped to his feet and came across to greet me.

'*Commissario* Armstrong, what a pleasure. Virgilio's told me so much about you.' He glanced at Oscar, who was looking at his new surroundings with interest. 'And this must be the famous Oscar – Virgilio told me he's an invaluable part of your investigative team.' He bent down to make a fuss of Oscar, who looked as though he could get used to being treated so royally.

I smiled back at Gressan. 'It's good to meet you, *Commissario*.

Thanks very much for putting in a word for me with Inspector Costey. She's an excellent detective and a credit to your force.'

'Pierre, please, call me Pierre. I'm glad you're impressed with Carmela; so am I. She'll be going off on maternity leave any day now – to be honest, she should be off already but she's far too stubborn – and we're going to struggle while she's away.' He gave me a wink and a little smile. 'If you want a job for a few months, just tell me.' He glanced at the clock on the wall. It was ten past eleven. 'I know she's waiting for you so she can go through all the stuff that's arrived from London but, if you have time, could I offer you lunch later on? I can guarantee you a good meal.'

'Thank you very much and, of course, do call me Dan. I'd be delighted to have lunch with you if you can spare the time. All right if I bring my four-legged friend?'

'Naturally. Now, Chanoux will show you through to Carmela's office. I'll see you later.'

'I look forward to it.'

Carmela was waiting in an office that also looked so very familiar to an old copper like me. Her desk was piled high with files, and one wall had been fitted with a large whiteboard and a similar-sized pinboard. This was covered in photos of the ufologists' camp above Montaz and the crime scene. I noticed that as well as a couple of photos of a barely recognisable blackened mass that was all that had remained of the victim, there were also two very different photos of Rick Brown or Browning. In one of these, he was very smartly dressed in an immaculate tuxedo at some showbiz gala or other, his arm draped around the bare shoulders of a very pretty young woman in an evening gown. In the other, he was kitted out like Indiana Jones with a leather jacket and a cowboy hat. He only needed a whip in his hand and the Ark of the Covenant beside him to complete the image. There was a step pyramid in the background that looked South American to me, but I'm no expert.

I took a good hard look at the man in the photos. Alice had described him as being very full of himself and certainly in these shots, he positively exuded self-confidence. He was a good-looking man with as fine a set of gleaming white teeth as Oscar – although quite possibly less genuine – and it was clear from his expression that he had been fully aware of his appearance. My mum would have described him as *flash* and I could imagine him appealing to members of the opposite sex – or, indeed, his own – and quite possibly arousing considerable jealous hostility among their husbands and boyfriends. Might his death have been a crime of passion? It wouldn't have surprised me but, if so, who had been so jealous as to resort to murder? I looked across at Carmela, who was just finishing a phone call. Maybe the background information from London would help us establish, if not a suspect, then at least some motive for his murder.

She put down the phone and picked up a familiar object from the jumble on her desk and waved it in the air. 'Come in and sit down. Sorry to have kept you waiting. Richard Brown's passport. The hotel had it so we now have definite identification, but there's nothing noteworthy in it; just a number of entry and exit stamps for a selection of countries, but nowhere sinister. At the hotel, they told me they have CCTV but the woman who knows how to work it was off this morning so they'll run off a copy of Tuesday's recordings and they say they'll hand it over to you as soon as possible'

I waved away the apology and sat down opposite her while Oscar wandered around the desk to say hello again. While she fondled his ears with one hand, she picked up a folder and passed it across to me with the other. 'See what you think. In the meantime, would you like a coffee or a tea?'

'A cappuccino would be great, thanks.'

She looked across at Chanoux, who was waiting expectantly by the door. 'A cappuccino for Dan and a decaf espresso for me, please.'

As he disappeared off down the corridor, I flicked through the pages of the report. Whether Paul had had something to do with compiling it or not, it had been meticulously done and I was impressed. A paragraph had been devoted to each of the ufologists and included date and place of birth, occupation, marital status and further information as appropriate. Many looked blameless, and by the time Chanoux returned with the coffees, I had distilled the list down to just a handful of names that I felt merited further investigation. These were Julian and Isabel, Libby, tattooed Don, Wayne the cameraman and, surprisingly, Maggie Vernon, Sandra's friend. As far as the others were concerned, I couldn't spot anything out of the ordinary.

Carmela pulled up a chair and sat down beside me while I talked her through it all. After skipping through the also-rans like Sybil and Wilfred and Bethany and Peter, I started with the remainder.

'None of the suspects has a criminal record apart from Donald Grimes. He was sentenced to four years for assault, of which he served just over two before being released on parole five years ago now. As far as the record shows, he's kept out of trouble since then, but it's clear he had, and maybe still has, a violent streak.'

Carmela was writing on her pad. 'Definitely needs to be interviewed again.'

'Julian Goodfellow spent fifteen years in the British Army, ending up as Major. He was commissioned into the Rifles and he served in Syria and Afghanistan. No commendations, but no black marks against him either. He appears to have been an average officer and, as part of an infantry unit, he probably saw his fair share of action. I imagine he wouldn't be afraid of bashing somebody over the head and setting fire to the body.' I nodded to myself. The fact that Julian had been in the army didn't come as a surprise and there was no doubt that this sort of background would have made him less squeamish than the average filmmaker. But could I see him as a murderer, particularly one prepared to pour petrol over a body and set fire to it?

'Anything about his TV company?'

'WKTTV sell their programmes to a number of networks in the UK and abroad.' I gave her a little grin. 'By the sound of it, he doesn't need the extra money he's raking in from the ufologists.'

'And his partner?'

'Julian Goodfellow's companion, Isabel Sanchez, is particularly interesting. She was born in the UK of Spanish parents and she's fifty-two. What's fascinating is that it appears that she was at RADA drama school in London thirty years ago at exactly the same time as Richard Brown or Browning.'

'So she was an actor too?'

'Yes, but she never made it into the big time. After a few years of bit parts and pantomimes, she married a Venezuelan millionaire who was murdered four years ago in Morocco by person or persons unknown – but there's a note here saying that the word at the time was that it was a gangland hit, possibly linked to narcotics. Anyway, he very kindly left her with a house in central London and a few million in the bank. Little else is known of her but the report says they're still checking.'

'And her connection with Julian Goodfellow?'

'They've worked together since he first set up the company eleven years ago. She acts as roving reporter and presenter and travels around the world with him. There's a link to her Facebook feed. Presumably, she's there to add a bit of glamour to the world of little green men. There's a link to YouTube so we can see for ourselves. No mention of how long she and Julian have been an item if, indeed, they are. They don't live together.'

'And the others?'

'Libby, that's Elizabeth Winter, age twenty-nine, has worked for Julian for just over a year. She got a first-class degree in media studies and went straight into television, starting at the bottom as a research assistant with local TV, then Sky, and gradually working her way up. This job with Julian's company looks like a massive step up for her. When I was talking to her yesterday, I got the feeling that maybe she was either afraid of Julian or that something was wrong there. I don't see how that ties in with Rick Browning, but I think she would be worth questioning more thoroughly. Anything's possible; maybe she came across Browning in her early years in television. Maybe he tried it on with her, who knows?'

Carmela was still scribbling. 'Definitely, who else?'

'Wayne O'Connell might be our man. He's only worked as a cameraman for WKTTV for six months and guess where he worked before that?' I supplied the answer for her. 'CosmosLink.'

'Well, well, the same company that Richard Brown worked for. That *is* interesting. We need to find out why he left. I wonder if he left under a cloud. Who knows? Maybe he crossed swords with Brown and when he recognised him again up at Montaz, he decided to settle accounts with him.'

I nodded in agreement. 'The last person of interest may be nothing at all but it's the one I know the least about. Her name is Margaret (Maggie) Vernon, and she's here with Sandra Wilson, the daughter of my friend, Inspector Wilson, in London. There's nothing negative about her in the report but what's caught my eye is that she works for yet another TV company, tvxUK. I've no idea what sort of programmes they make but it would be worth finding out. Wouldn't it be interesting if they, too, were involved with

UFOs? I'm happy to check that online before you come up to interview these people again.'

'Thanks, Dan, that's a great help. The interviews had better be tomorrow morning. I'm afraid I have a prior engagement this afternoon.' She shot me a little smile. 'I have to go for an antenatal check-up with the midwife at the hospital.'

'If there's anything else I can do for you, just say the word. I'm happy to help.' And the fact of the matter was that I really was happy to help. This all felt just like old times. Being a private investigator can get quite repetitive and, to be honest, it sometimes feels pretty sleazy, sneaking around, checking up on other people's dirty little secrets. Being involved in a real police murder investigation was meat and drink to me. Thought of meat and drink reminded me of my lunch invitation and I told Carmela about it. Her smile broadened.

'I wish I could come with you. Pierre's great company and what he doesn't know about policing – or, in fact, just about anything – here in the valley isn't worth knowing.' She finished her now barely lukewarm decaf and heaved herself to her feet with a heartfelt sigh. I gave her a sympathetic look.

'Is this your first?'

She nodded. 'And I'll be glad when the baby comes. I feel like a whale, my ankles are swollen, and for some reason, I can't stop eating sardines. The cats will be following me around soon. What about you? Have you got kids?'

'One daughter but she's thirty now. She's getting married next year so I may find myself a grandfather before long.'

'Does Oscar know he might have competition for your affection?'

I glanced down at him as he rubbed his head affectionately against Carmela's leg. 'He's a naturally friendly dog. He'll take it in his stride.'

14

THURSDAY AFTERNOON

Pierre Gressan wasn't wrong about it being a good lunch. He led me through the stone-paved streets of the old town of Aosta, past the remains of the two-thousand-year-old Roman fortress, until we reached a very ancient, low, stone building roofed with massive, rough-hewn slabs of stone. The structure looked as though it had always been there and the ancient, carved, oak front door wouldn't have looked out of place on a castle. Inside, the restaurant was already over half full although it was only just past noon, and a wonderful aroma of cooking filled the air. A waiter showed us to our table and the proprietor, who clearly knew Pierre well, came over to shake our hands and tell us what today's specials were. I was fascinated to hear the two men talking to each other in the local patois, which sounded more French than Italian although, even with my French A level gained back in the mists of time, I barely understood a word.

Pierre glanced across at me and addressed me in Italian. 'Are you feeling hungry?'

For a moment, I could have sworn I saw Oscar nod his head. When it comes to food, he's a polyglot as well as a glutton. 'Definitely. I'm happy to eat anything. I've never been to Aosta before so, as you're the local, you choose.'

A short conversation in patois ensued and after the restaurateur had gone off, Pierre told me what lay ahead. 'You can't come to Aosta without trying some of our local specialities so I've ordered *fonduta* followed by carbonade of beef with polenta. I don't know what plans you have for dinner tonight, but you probably won't need much after this.'

He wasn't joking. When the first course arrived in scalding-hot little cast-iron pots it looked for all the world like Swiss fondue, but the taste was subtly different. As well as cubes of bread to dip in it, we were also served a selection of vegetables ranging from small potatoes to chunks of broccoli. Pierre told me that the secret of this dish was the Fontina cheese – I had already worked out that Fontina was the valley's most famous export – and that this was mixed with eggs and slivers of truffles. The result was excellent and we drank a lovely local wine with it.

We chatted as we ate. He asked me about life at Scotland Yard and seemed mildly surprised when I told him that police work over there really wasn't that different from police work over here. I told him about my new venture as Dan Armstrong PI and he expressed interest.

'I'm going to retire next year so if you ever need a pair of hands up here in the Alps, just say the word. I'd be delighted to help out.'

'You never know. I'm not here on official business this time but, now that my agency's beginning to get known, I'm sometimes being asked to go outside my usual Tuscany area. I'll certainly remember that. Carmela told me you know everything about policing in the valley.'

'When you've been doing it as long as I have, you get to know most of what's going on.'

I was just finishing my *fonduta* – and handing the last

remaining pieces of bread down to the ever-hungry dog at my feet
– when my phone rang. It was Paul in London and he had news.

'I've been doing a bit more digging on your ufologists and I've
come up with a couple of new bits of information. I've spoken to
the head of HR at CosmosLink TV and she provided me with a
fascinating bit of news. Wayne O'Connell was fired because he
assaulted another member of staff. Feel like hazarding a guess as to
who that might have been?'

'Not our very own Rick Brown by any chance?'

'The very same. The word at the time was that the assault was
over a woman, but the HR lady couldn't tell me any more than
that.'

'We're planning on sitting down for a serious talk to Mr O'Connell tomorrow morning so this will be very useful ammunition.
Thanks a lot, Paul.'

'And there's more. DC Mallory, one of our new recruits – after
your time, Dan – knows somebody who works at CosmosLink TV
and she's promised to have a drink with him tomorrow lunchtime
and see what she can find out in the way of gossip – the sort of stuff
the HR person wouldn't talk about. So watch this space; I might
have more for you on O'Connell or on the victim.'

'Terrific, that'll be a great help. I'm pleased to report that
Sandra's doing fine, but I wonder if you could check out her friend,
Maggie Vernon. She apparently works for a TV company called
tvxUK. There's probably nothing in it, but I'd like it checked.
Could you see if she has any connection with Rick Brown or, for
that matter, with Julian's company, WKTTV? I know she and
Sandra are good friends so I don't want to make things awkward
unless I have something concrete to go on.'

'Leave it to me and thanks, Dan, I really appreciate you helping
out like this.'

'Any time, buddy.'

One thing was now clear. When I had asked if anybody up at the camp had known the victim, they had all shaken their heads. It was rapidly emerging that more than one of them had been lying and, if so, why?

Any further conjecture was interrupted by the arrival of the waiter with a huge plateful of beef stew served on a bed of polenta, but not just any polenta. I quite like the stuff, but I'm not normally wild about it. It's made from maize and has the consistency of pureed potatoes and it often tastes a bit bland. Today's dish was anything but bland as it had been laced with Fontina – inevitably – as well as a local blue cheese, and the result was an extremely tasty mix of flavours. In fact, it could have made an excellent dish all on its own, but today, it was liberally heaped with beef stew in gravy and the combination, apart from probably supplying me with more than my regulation calorific intake for the whole day, was wonderful. As we ate, I told Pierre what I had just heard from Paul and he nodded sagely.

'*Cherchez la femme.* You wait, it sounds to me as though the victim might have been murdered out of jealousy. Your interview with the cameraman should be interesting.'

I felt the same way.

Somehow, I managed to find room after all the polenta and beef for an exceptional panna cotta with flambéed fruits of the forest in syrup that probably added another thousand calories to the meal, but I was past caring. It wasn't every day I had the opportunity to eat so well and I took advantage of it. Besides, I told myself, Oscar and I could walk it off in the mountains later.

After lunch – for which Pierre insisted on paying – and the inevitable shot of remarkably good grappa, I thanked him most warmly and went for a walk around the town. Aosta was in so many ways a winter town with shop after shop selling skis, ski clothes, hiking and climbing gear as well as numerous bars –

including the obligatory 'British' pub – all of which advertised *vin brûlé*. Today definitely wasn't *vin brûlé* weather and I found myself avoiding the direct sunlight and hugging the shade not just for the sake of my dog. Mind you, with all those calories coursing through my veins, it was inevitable that I would be feeling warm.

I thoroughly enjoyed my visit to the town but I was quite happy to do a bit of shopping and then drive back up to Montaz later on and check into the Albergo Italia. They gave me a comfortable room with a little balcony, and the view down over the village to the valley below and the mountains beyond was delightful. I stood there, leaning on the railings, and breathed deeply. At my feet, Oscar stuck his nose through the iron bars and did the same. The clean mountain air was refreshing. There was ample room for me to set up Oscar's bed by the window and I muttered a little prayer that he would decide to sleep in it rather than try and climb into my bed with me.

Before settling down to check the Internet as I had promised Carmela, I thought I would take Oscar for a walk around the village and give him a chance to have a run in the surrounding forest. As I had thought, it really was a very small village and I had seen all of it, including the tiny little church, within fifteen minutes, so we headed a bit further afield into the trees and spent a pleasant half-hour walking along a network of paths with Oscar constantly on the lookout for sticks or pine cones for me to throw for him to retrieve. Once again, if there hadn't been a murderer on the loose, it would have been idyllic.

Back in my room, I pulled out the iPad and did a bit of online research. I started by looking up the company where Sandra's friend, Maggie, worked and what I discovered came as quite a surprise. It took barely a few seconds on the tvxUK website for me to realise that the company did not, after all, specialise in producing extra-terrestrial investigations, but a very different kind of programme entirely.

Maggie worked for a company producing adult movies.

The report from London had only indicated that she worked for tvxUK but it hadn't given any clue as to her position in the company. I did a search of the pretty explicit video covers on display – purely in the interests of the investigation, of course – but none of the women in varying stages of undress were Maggie. Of course, this didn't necessarily mean she wasn't a porn star, but it made it more likely that she occupied a position in the admin or production side of the process. I wondered whether Sandra knew the true nature of her friend's employers. Still, whether her job involved taking her clothes off or not, as far as this murder investigation was concerned, it came as a relief to find that she had no apparent connection with either WKTTV or CosmosLink.

The other bit of research I undertook was to check the Facebook page belonging to Isabel Sanchez. Almost all of the posts and photos were about how successful her career was proving to be. A check on YouTube made it clear that she certainly didn't appear to have any hesitation about showing off her physical attributes and for a moment, it occurred to me that she could probably have made a successful career for herself in front of the cameras at tvxUK. However, apart from confirming that she quite clearly had an actor's ego, the Facebook posts and videos didn't shed any more light on her and, while she still remained a person of interest, there didn't appear to be anything much to quiz her about.

15

THURSDAY EVENING

Pierre was right. When the evening came, I really didn't feel much like eating a full meal so I decided to skip dinner. I drove up to the camp to hand over the milk and the eggs I had bought for Val and on the way, I stopped off at Il Convento to buy some more supplies for myself. It didn't take much to persuade me to have a cold beer. This very soon developed into a second beer and a focaccia sandwich with goats' cheese and roast aubergine. My ex-wife often accused me of being greedy, but greed is a very relative thing. Labradors are in a class of their own, but from the look on Oscar's face tonight, it was pretty clear that he thought he occupied the moral high ground for once.

I sat outside and enjoyed the last of the evening sun and, while I was sitting there, I got a phone call. This time, it had nothing to do with the case. It was Melissa, my editor at the publishers in London, and she was calling about my second whodunnit. I had sent her the first draft a couple of weeks earlier and had been waiting anxiously for her verdict. She didn't waste any time.

'Dan, I loved it.'

A wave of relief swept over me. 'You did?'

'Absolutely, it's every bit as good as the first.'

The relief was followed by a wave of euphoria and I took a big swig of beer to celebrate as she continued extolling its virtues.

'I have a couple of suggestions for minor tweaks and I've put them into an email for you but I just wanted to call you to say how much I enjoyed it.'

'It was very kind of you to call, Melissa. Thanks a lot.'

'How're things in Florence? It's pouring with rain here; what sort of weather have you got down there in gorgeous Tuscany?'

'I'm not actually in Tuscany at the moment but I imagine the weather's like it is here: bright and sunny. I'm up in the Alps investigating a murder.'

'Wow, how exciting! Who's been killed?'

I mentioned that a British actor had been murdered and it quickly emerged that she had been following the case closely, and there was a reason for this. 'I was sorry when I heard the news of Rick's death, but not that sorry. I'm good friends with his ex-wife, Veronica, and he treated her appallingly.'

'In what way?' Although I had a feeling I knew what the answer was going to be before she said it.

'He couldn't keep his hands off other women. He led her a terrible life and I don't know how she managed to stick it as long as she did. Certainly, divorcing him was the best thing she's ever done.'

My mind was turning over any possible benefit I could get out of being able to question somebody who knew so much background to the victim but, before I could think of a question, Melissa came up with a fascinating snippet of information, albeit incomplete.

'She divorced him a few years ago now, but it's pretty clear that he just carried on breaking other women's hearts after Veronica threw him out. Not that long ago, just a few months or so, I read about some poor woman who allegedly took her own life because of him. The Internet was full of stories that Rick had been her lover, and when she found out he'd been unfaithful to her, she couldn't handle it and killed herself.'

'You can't remember her name, can you?'

'No, but I bet I know who could. Your friend Jess, the journalist that I met at your book signing the other month. She struck me as having her ear very close to the ground. I'm sure if you asked her, she'd be able to dig up the information.'

'That's a brilliant idea, Melissa. Have you ever thought of going into detective work?'

She laughed and we chatted some more before she rang off, leaving me feeling extremely happy at the news that she liked book number two, and fascinated about the news of the broken-hearted former lover of Rick Brown. Might that have something to do with this case?

I immediately called Jess Barnes and she sounded pleased to hear from me.

'Hello, handsome, how's life in Tuscany? I'm still waiting for my invitation to visit, you know.'

'I'm not sure how happy Keith would be if you came swanning across to see me.' I had met her husband a few times and I knew that they had a very happy marriage and a pair of young twins who kept them on their toes. I had known Jess for over twenty years and we had a bond of mutual respect. For a journalist, she had an unusual amount of human decency, and in my experience, that's not always that common in that profession. 'I wonder if you could dig up a bit of information for me.' I went on to tell her what Melissa had just told me and her response was predictably helpful.

'I vaguely remember the story. I'll see what I can find and I'll send it across. It'll have to be tomorrow as Keith and I are on our way out – just the two of us for a change, no kids!'

As she was talking, it occurred to me that I could probably have asked Alice Turner for her help. She was here after all, and I felt pretty sure that, as an investigative journalist for one of the tabloids, she might even have the facts at her fingertips. Mind you, I thought to myself, reverting to chief-inspector mode, she was also still potentially a suspect so it was wiser to leave her out of the investigation.

Jess and I had a good chat and I was able to pass on the news that my publishers appeared happy with the second book in the series. I promised her that if I came over to the UK for another book signing when that one launched, I would take her and the family out for a good meal to say thank you for managing to get me that amazing article in *The Sunday Times* that had given the book a terrific boost.

I had only just finished the call when I heard my name and looked up to see Wilfred and Sybil coming along the drive towards me. It looked as though they had walked down from the camp so that confirmed that they were fit for their age – whatever that was.

'Hello, Dan, had a good day?'

I decided to tell them a version of the truth. 'A busy day, helping the police with a bit of interpreting.' I feigned frustration. 'I came here for a holiday and to see for myself what everybody's been seeing in the skies up here. Anything new since last night?'

Sybil answered for both of them. 'Nothing. The only activity seems to be at night. I suppose it's so that they can get about unobserved.'

I couldn't help pointing out the problem with that argument. 'But surely if they don't want to be seen, they shouldn't carry lights.' Before they had to answer that, I indicated the spare seats at my table. It occurred to me that it might be a good idea now that I'd got these two on their own to ask a few questions on a more informal basis. 'Can I get you a drink? If you've walked down from the camp, you might be ready for a cold beer like me.'

They sat down and I attracted Conrad's attention. Wilfred ordered a beer and Sybil let me persuade her to have a glass of white wine. We chatted about generalities for a few minutes while the drinks arrived and then I brought the subject around to the murder.

'Isn't it awful about the murder? What or who do you think's behind it?'

Wilfred glanced around and then leant towards me, keeping his voice low. 'There are a lot of... you know... foreigners here at this hostel or whatever it is. You must have seen them. What if one of them decided to kill Nick and rob him? It's the kind of thing that sort of people might do.'

I restrained myself. Conrad and his companions struck me as decent people and the implied racism in old Wilfred's voice saddened me. After fighting against racist officers within the force over and over again during my time at the Met, it was disappointing – and downright distasteful – to hear it being voiced by this apparently harmless old duffer. Still, picking a fight with Wilfred wouldn't help the investigation so I ignored the odious implications of his suggestion and shook my head.

'The inspector says it can't have been aggravated theft. She's checked the victim's bank cards and nothing's been taken, and the pathologist found a Rolex watch still on his wrist. Everybody knows how much they cost, and surely a thief wouldn't have overlooked that.'

'Is it true that Nick Green wasn't his real name? The boys up at the camp say that the Internet's full of talk of it being a chap called Rick Browning.'

Sybil's question put me on the spot and I had to stop and think before replying. As far as I knew, Carmela hadn't informed the ufologists of his true identity yet, but it was inevitable that, just I had learnt it from my daughter, some of the people at the camp would have heard it for themselves. I decided to confirm their supposition.

'Yes, the news came through first thing this morning, I believe. Browning was his stage name – does it mean anything to you?'

Wilfred nodded. 'Oh yes, he's... he was very well known in the world of investigations into extra-terrestrial life. He had his own programme on Discovery Channel and several other channels. He was a believer, just like us. It's ironic that he was killed by one of his beloved extra-terrestrials.'

I got the feeling Wilfred was losing the plot but I did my best to keep my voice level and cordial as I tried to put him right. 'But he wasn't killed by an alien spacecraft, Wilfred. He was murdered. That's definite.'

Wilfred looked sceptical. 'That's what they always say. Nobody ever wants to believe us.' He picked up his glass and did his magical disappearing drink act and half of his glass of beer vanished into the recesses of his beard. Setting the glass back down again, he fixed me with a conspiratorial stare and I stared back in amazement. There wasn't even any froth on his beard. How did he do it? I didn't have more time to ponder the conundrum as he was still on the offensive. 'We know the truth, Dan. Remember that, whatever the police try to tell you.'

There was no point arguing so I just nodded sagely. It was noticeably less chilly this evening and we spent the next hour or so chatting as the sun gradually disappeared from sight behind the distant mountains and darkness began to fall. I found that if we avoided racism and UFOs, Wilfred was actually quite good company, although, of the two of them, Sybil was the one who did most of the talking. I didn't really learn much more about the dynamics of the group but one little snippet of information interested me when she came out with it.

'Of course, we're all very upset at what happened and it's affected Julian and Isabel in particular. I heard the two of them having a right old shouting match this afternoon, which is unusual for them. Normally, they're cool, calm and collected but, boy, did they have a row!'

'I wonder what sparked that off.'

Wilfred shook his head sadly. 'Just nervous tension, I expect. We're all on edge. After all, we may be closer now to discovering proof of alien life than ever before and the last thing we need is a bunch of police officers tramping about the place, disturbing everything.'

When it was quite dark and the stars were already starting to twinkle overhead, I gave the two of them a lift back up to the camp and delivered the rations to Val, who was, as ever, positioned by the fire. Most of the others were there as well but as I drank my way through yet another mug of tea, they gradually began to get up and start making their way up to the top of Mont Saint Georges in readiness for tonight's light show.

I went back to the van and gave Oscar his evening meal, which disappeared in a matter of seconds as usual, and checked my emails. Sure enough, there was one from Melissa about my new book and along with it, she had returned the manuscript with various comments, additions and subtractions that she had made. Although she had indicated in her call that she had very few suggestions, in fact there was quite a lot to go through and it was late by the time I finally gave up for the night. I looked over my shoulder to where Oscar was fast asleep in his basket and threw out a suggestion.

'Fancy a walk, dog?'

One eye opened and then the other and then, barely a second

later, he jumped to his feet and shook himself. The magic word had worked yet again.

I collected a jumper just in case, and this time remembered to pick up my binoculars before setting off up the track towards the observation post. As we climbed, I pulled out my phone, called Anna and gave her a report on my day so far. She told me about her day and then passed on a message to me from her aunt.

'Zia Menca says she knows those two UFO TV companies and she'll send you an email tomorrow, but she told me to tell you that the one belonging to Julian Whatsisname doesn't have a particularly good reputation for telling the truth.'

'Considering the book he's written and his programmes are called *We Know the Truth,* that's a bit rich, but it comes as no surprise. He certainly appears to be milking the death of Brown as hard as he can. Does she think he makes stuff up on purpose to pad out his programmes?'

'Exactly. Anyway, she says she'll know more tomorrow.'

When I got up to the observation post, I found most of the ufologists already there. It was a beautiful night and, without the light pollution of the big cities, the whole sky was studded with stars and I could see what looked like Venus just above the horizon. I sat down and reached for my binoculars while Oscar wandered about, graciously accepting pats and strokes from the assembled crowd.

'Hi, Dan, I missed you at dinner.' Alice came over and perched on the rock beside me. 'Were you doing anything interesting?'

I told her how I had opted for a snack rather than a big meal and how I had ended up at the convent chatting to Wilfred and Sybil. To my surprise, I saw the elderly couple sitting a bit further along from me, chatting to Julian, who had his binoculars at the ready. It was almost midnight and after their walk down to the convent earlier, I had expected them to be tucked up in bed. These two certainly were fit, but of course they had had the incentive of potential inter-galactic contact to look forward to. I let my eyes stray over the assembled throng and saw that we had an almost full house. As far as I could see, the only ufologists missing tonight were Libby, Isabel and Val, although her taciturn daughter, Millie, was up here.

Conscious that the others were probably listening, I gave Alice the same story that I'd given to Wilfred and Sybil and it was clear from the reactions around me that Brown's true identity was now common knowledge. Given that this was no longer a secret, I tried doing a bit of fishing.

'What I don't understand is what he was doing up here with you if he worked for a rival company.'

Predictably, Julian was the first to react. 'Industrial espionage, or maybe even industrial sabotage! He was either trying to steal our ideas or to screw up what we're doing here. So typical of the devious little weasel. I couldn't believe it when I heard who he was and that he'd been here, but it's typical of a slimy toad like that. He's been copying us for years and he even popped up last year when we were filming at Chichen Itza. I literally bumped into him. He wasn't in disguise that time and when I accused him of deliberately tailing us, he just laughed.' Julian snorted. 'But to come here and try to pass himself off as an innocent member of the group, it's despicable!'

It came as no surprise to find that there was no love lost between the two men, but just how deep did the animosity spread? Deep enough for murder?

'I must say that I'm sorry he's dead. I, for one, definitely enjoyed his programmes.' All eyes turned towards Val's daughter, of all people. It was so unusual to hear her say anything that hearing her come out with something so controversial in the present company was a genuine surprise. This even stopped Julian in his tracks – but only for a moment or two.

'His programmes are pretty slick, I'll give you that, Millie, but of course that's more down to the production team than down to him. What rankles with me is the fact that they just so patently copy our stuff. It's unprofessional and it's reprehensible!' Maybe realising that he was coming across a bit too bitter about some-body who'd just been bludgeoned to death, he adopted a slightly more conciliatory tone. 'Naturally, on a personal level I'm sorry the man's dead but, professionally speaking, he's no great loss.' With this, he stood up and wandered off along the path that led towards the next peak, leaving me wondering how sorry he really was.

I chatted to Alice and to a couple of the others on and off for the next hour or so until it was almost one o'clock. Just as I was seriously considering calling it a day and heading back down to the hotel for a good night's sleep, there was a chorus of muted voices and all eyes turned to the north towards the Matterhorn. I picked up the binoculars and scoured the sky until a light came into view. I screwed the focus wheel until I could see it more clearly but all that was revealed was a very bright, white light at high altitude. It was hard to tell how high but the extra-terrestrial vehicle – if that was what it was – was too far away for even the best binoculars to identify it beyond the glare of its lights. As for the cameras and telescopes, the thing was moving so fast, I could see them struggling to follow it. And then, like the previous night, it zigzagged sharply and dived down to disappear from sight behind the mountains.

I looked across at my companions, who were chattering animatedly, quite obviously convinced that they had just seen living proof that UFOs did exist. I, on the other hand, had a feeling that what we had just seen was much more likely to turn out to have a terrestrial origin.

16

FRIDAY MORNING

My first night sharing the hotel room with Oscar was not without incident. At around four o'clock in the morning, I awoke feeling very hot and found a heavy and far from fragrant body pressed tightly against me, and a battle of wills then ensued. I heaved him off and led him across to his basket and wagged my finger at him until he got the message and stayed there. I then went back to bed and closed my eyes but five minutes later, found I had canine company all over again. This continued for twenty minutes or so until, finally, Oscar must have realised that there was no future in it for him and he left me alone.

After meticulously brushing any incriminating black dog hairs off the bed, I had an early breakfast and drove up to the camp at seven-thirty to find it still quiet, so presumably everybody was sleeping off the late night of stargazing. I parked the van, and Oscar and I walked down through the trees to Il Convento where we were to meet up with Carmela and Sergeant Fournier at eight. Today, the sky was cloudy and I had a feeling it might rain before dark, but the air was noticeably less chilly than yesterday morning and we sat outside while we drank coffee and talked.

The detectives' breakfast and my cappuccino were interrupted by a call to Carmela. I saw at once that something was wrong and as soon as the call ended, I raised an eyebrow. 'Trouble?'

'Up at the camp. One of the group's disappeared.'

'Really, who?' I found myself praying it wasn't Paul's sister.

'Elizabeth Winter. She didn't sleep in her room at the hotel last night and there's no sign of her at the camp this morning.'

'Libby's gone AWOL? Could it be she has a guilty conscience and she's made a break for it?'

Sergeant Fournier caught the inspector's eye and gave her a little grin as he pointed skywards. 'Alternatively, are you thinking what I'm thinking?'

Carmela shook her head firmly. 'No, I most certainly am not. There will be no alien abductions on my watch. We need to get up there straight away.'

I nodded. 'I couldn't agree more. I'd be surprised if she really has run away. She didn't look too cheerful but she certainly didn't give any hint of wanting to leave. I suppose it could be she's just gone off with a man. She is a very attractive woman, after all.'

'I hope that's what's happened.' The inspector drained her decaf and pulled herself to her feet. 'You and I had better not show up together, so why don't you walk back up the way you came and I'll muddle through until you arrive? Fournier can do a bit of interpreting until you get there. Okay, Fournier?'

He shot me a rueful look. 'I'll do my best, Inspector, but you know...'

I was still processing the information about Libby. What if she hadn't just left but had been assaulted or worse? Who might it have been: her boss, with whom she wasn't entirely comfortable, the cameraman who maybe lusted after her or even Brown's murderer covering his or her tracks? Had she seen or heard something on Tuesday night? I stood up as well. 'I'll get back to camp as soon as I can. Who reported Libby missing?'

'The call came from the owner of the hotel in Montaz: a Luigi Arnad.'

'The same man who reported Brown's death. Useful guy to know, although I wouldn't trust him as far as I could throw him.'

When I got to the camp, I found the place crawling with activity. A little white Fiat belonging to the local police was parked there alongside Carmela's squad car. It looked as though all the ufologists were up and about and Val was handing out mugs of tea to all and sundry. I spotted Alice talking to the Pirates of the Caribbean and I went over to talk to her. There was a worried expression on her face when she told me what had happened.

'I usually have breakfast with Libby so when she didn't come down, I texted her to see if all was well. There was no answer so I checked with the reception desk and they told me she hadn't come back last night. Her key was still hanging on the board behind the counter and I was worried. I jumped in the car and came straight up to the camp. When I got up here, I checked with Julian and he said she'd left at about nine last night and he hadn't seen her since. The thing is that her car isn't at the hotel and it isn't here. She's just disappeared into thin air.'

'Do you think she might have done a runner?'

'I can't see why she would have done. I'm sure she had nothing to do with the murder.'

'I'll ask if the inspector's sent somebody to check her room in case her stuff's gone.'

I could see the inspector with Julian outside his motorhome so Oscar and I went over to help. Carmela gave me a little wave as she spotted me and addressed me formally for the sake of any onlookers who might secretly understand a bit of Italian.

'Signor Armstrong, I'm afraid I need your help again. We have a missing person, Elizabeth Winter, one of this gentleman's employees. I need to know when he last saw her.'

I nodded and concentrated my attention on Julian, who was looking most concerned. 'Libby's gone off?' I saw him nod. 'When did you last see her?'

'Just after nine last night. Along with Isabel, she and I were doing some in-fill and voiceovers to go with the film I'm making about the events up here and we were occupied with that from about six-thirty onwards. When we finished, Libby said she was going back to her hotel for something to eat and then straight to bed. Isabel and I had a bite to eat in our camper and then went up to the observation point where you saw me. I haven't seen her since.'

Dutifully, I translated for Carmela's benefit and she waited until I'd finished before commenting.

'So that's almost exactly twelve hours ago. Do you think she might have gone away, maybe even back to the UK?'

Julian shook his head. 'Definitely not. She has a job to do here and she's always been most reliable.'

I translated for Carmela and then told her what Alice had told me. The inspector immediately pulled out her phone. 'Hello, Chanoux. Where are you? Good. I need you to stop off at the Albergo Italia. Elizabeth Winter has disappeared and I need you to check her room. See if her things are still there and see if the hotel is holding her passport. If there's anything suspicious or if there's any clue as to where she might have gone, call me straight back.'

We were still talking to Julian without getting any more useful information out of him when the inspector's phone rang. It was a short call from Officer Chanoux and the gist of it was that the constable had found Libby's passport still at reception and he confirmed that all her belongings appeared to be in her room. The inspector looked grim.

'Right, that would appear to show that she hasn't run off, so it could be that something's happened to her. We'll start a search for her immediately. The first thing we need to find is the car. It may still be around here somewhere. What sort is it?'

Julian provided the information that it was a rented, white Fiat 500 and the police were sent off back down the road with instructions to check every parking area or track leading into the woods. It can't have been much more than five minutes later that the call came in. Carmela and I were in the tent where we had been deciding what questions we needed to put to Julian and Wayne O'Connell about their relations with Richard Brown, but that was immediately put on hold. She stood up.

'The car's been found only about five hundred metres from here. Apparently, there's a track leading off the road to the right as we look at it, and her car was parked just a stone's throw from the road. No sign of Elizabeth... Libby, so we need to start a serious search.'

I followed her out of the tent and across to where the ufologists had gathered around the campfire. They all looked up with interest as Carmela held up her hand for silence and I translated.

'Libby's car has been found barely ten minutes on foot from here and we're organising a search party. Who'll volunteer to help?'

Everybody raised their hands and she nodded. 'Right, four teams. One of my men in each. Signor Armstrong, maybe you'll be good enough to lead one of the teams. Sergeant Fournier, you assign search zones to each team and I'll get Chanoux to take me down the road in a squad car.' She waved apologetically towards her tummy. 'The midwife told me not to do too much walking. My officers can communicate with me by radio or phone.'

A few minutes later, we all set off. I took my little group consisting of Julian and Isabel and headed over to the northern side of the road where we started making our way along a maze of animal tracks in the direction of Libby's car. Another group was sent off to the left while another went further to the right of us and the others went on uphill before turning off on either side of the road so as to circle back to the car through the trees. Below us, we could hear the voices of the police already searching the immediate area around the car. Julian and Isabel both looked concerned but not nearly as troubled as some of the others at the camp had been. Wayne, the cameraman, in particular had looked distraught. As we walked down through the trees, I took advantage of having the pair on their own to ask some searching questions.

'Tell me, at what point did you recognise that Tuesday night's victim was a man called Richard Brown or Rick Browning?'

Julian actually stopped dead and turned towards me. I kept my eyes on his face, trying to assess his reaction. 'I didn't recognise him at all. The first I heard of it being him was last night.'

'Are you both quite sure about that?' Although I found myself tending to believe him, I kept my attention firmly not only on his face but also on that of Isabel, his partner. She remained expressionless at first, while Julian's reaction was one of outrage. Clearly, his feelings towards the victim hadn't improved overnight.

'I still can't believe that little rat had the nerve, the cheek, to dress himself up in bandages and came up here to spy on me and my team. It's reprehensible, isn't it, Isabel?'

My eyes moved back to Isabel and for the first time, I spotted what might have been sympathy on her face. 'When Crispin and Geoffrey told me who it was yesterday, I didn't believe them at first. I... we've met him numerous times and I find it amazing that he managed to fool us all like that.' Her voice dropped to little more than a whisper. 'And now, of course, he's dead.'

If I hadn't been told that Browning and Julian's company were at daggers drawn, I would have believed that she was genuinely saddened by this turn of events. My suspicious nature immediately made me question whether she and Julian maybe hadn't both been on the same page as far as Rick Browning was concerned. I couldn't miss the anger on Julian's face, but Isabel was harder to read.

However, before I could go any further with the questioning, there was the sound of a whistle and clear shouts of *'Eccola qui.'* Here she is.

I instructed Julian and Isabel to return to camp. They were reluctant but I managed to insist. As soon as they had disappeared back up the track, I sprinted in the direction of the whistle with Oscar running joyfully ahead of me, convinced that this was some sort of game.

We emerged from the undergrowth to find Libby's slim body sprawled face down on the ground with a horrific wound to the side of her head and blood staining the ground all around. Standing at her feet, rooted to the spot, was a young, uniformed constable of the local police accompanied by Crispin and Geoffrey along with Sandra and Maggie. I ran up to the officer and caught him by the arm, spinning him towards me.

'For Christ's sake, take these people away and send them back to the camp. And make sure you keep anybody else from seeing her like this. Call the inspector and get other officers to help put up a cordon.'

I had to grab Sandra by the arm and shake her horror-stricken gaze from the body and push her back in the direction of the camp along with Maggie. The young policeman finally pulled himself together and collected the apparently equally stunned Geoffrey and Crispin and led them all away. Not a word was spoken. I knelt down alongside the body and let my hand rest against the cold skin of Libby's throat to feel her carotid artery. To my surprise, in spite of the gruesome wound, I felt a pulse. She was still alive but clearly deeply unconscious.

I pulled my jumper from around my waist and stretched it over Libby's shoulders and cleared some of the moss and dead leaves from her face so she could breathe more easily. I was just reaching for my phone to call Carmela when running footsteps announced the arrival of Sergeant Fournier. He stopped dead when he saw the body and I was quick to tell him what I'd just discovered.

'She's alive, Fournier, but seriously injured. Get the paramedics here as soon as possible. She's in a really bad way. Can you give me your jacket? We need to warm her up. She's like a block of ice.'

The next thing I saw was Oscar, emitting little whimpering sounds, making his way slowly over to Libby's side where he lay down tight against her, adding his body heat to the covers on top of her. I stretched out my hand and stroked his head as he looked up at me with deep concern in his big, brown eyes. He really is a very good dog.

Carmela and Chanoux arrived a few minutes later and they also contributed items of clothing to the growing pile on top of Libby as we desperately tried to raise her core temperature. From the look of her, she had quite possibly been here all night and, although the night-time temperature had risen over recent days, she had to be close to hypothermic by now. The ambulance arrived barely half an hour later, which was impressive, considering the tortuous road to get up here. The paramedics took over and Oscar and I were relieved of our duties.

As they set to work on Libby, I went over to Carmela. She was standing against the bonnet of the patrol car, resting heavily against it as she supported her big baby bump with both hands. I gave her a sympathetic look.

'I didn't get a chance to ask earlier. What did the midwife say yesterday? All well, I hope.'

She gave me a little smile. 'Everything's fine and normal but, to be perfectly honest, she told me to stop work, but I can't duck out in the middle of a murder investigation.' She ran a weary hand through her hair. 'Thanks for asking.'

'If I were your boss, I'd send you home right now. Your health is more important than any investigation.'

She reached over and caught hold of my arm for a moment, fixing me with a firm stare. 'But you're not my boss, and if you mention a word of this to Pierre, I swear I'll arrest you as an accessory to murder.'

I smiled back. 'Okay, I promise, but just try and take it easy. All right? Anyway, the good news is that Libby's still alive, but she's in a very bad way. From what I could hear of the paramedics, her life's on the line.'

'Considering the state of that head wound, I'm amazed she's alive at all.'

I nodded. 'And I wouldn't mind betting that the person who hit her went off convinced she was dead or at least that she was dying. Who do we think did it?'

'I would lay money on it being one of the ufologists, wouldn't you? The car wasn't touched. It's unlocked and the keys and her handbag with her phone and purse are still in it. She doesn't appear to have been molested in any way so that all rules out an opportunistic murder. Like I say, it has to be one of the group.'

'I'm with you on that. Do we think it was the same person who killed Brown? Might Libby have witnessed something she shouldn't have done, maybe?'

'The two attacks have to be connected, surely, so I suppose we have to treat it as most probably the work of the same person. After all, the *modus operandi* was the same. I'll get somebody from the forensic team to go to the hospital to talk to the surgeons who'll be working on her. We need to find out what hit her and when.'

I nodded approvingly. 'Just an idea, but might it be worth not revealing that she's still alive, at least for now? That way the would-be murderer might be lulled into a false sense of security and it would avoid anybody thinking about going to the hospital to finish the job.'

'Good idea. I'll tell my officers.' She caught my eye. 'Of course, it could well be that the killer will get his or her wish after all. She doesn't look good.' At that moment, the paramedics had emerged from the trees carrying Libby on a stretcher. She was swathed in dressings and heaped with blankets and the only bits of her skin that were visible were as white as snow. They slid her into the ambulance and while the driver climbed in and started the engine, the female paramedic came across to Carmela.

'She's very weak, but she's still alive. That's all I can tell you.'

'Any idea when she was attacked?'

'I'm no pathologist, but we both reckon she'd been there all night.'

Carmela gave the woman a smile. 'Thanks for your help. Here's hoping...'

The ambulance reversed into the track, turned, and set off back down the hill again, blue lights flashing. Meanwhile, I was doing a bit of calculating.

'Julian claimed that Libby went off in her car at just after nine last night. Assuming some of the others can corroborate that and that the paramedics are right that she'd been lying there all night, I reckon the murder attempt might have happened pretty soon after that, maybe even immediately after nine. How's this for a scenario? Her would-be killer is waiting at the side of the road and he or she flags her down on a pretext, gets her into the trees and hits her with what they believed to be a deadly blow.'

'And a woman on her own is unlikely to have stopped for somebody she didn't know, particularly in the dark. That makes it all the more likely that her attacker is one of the ufologists.'

I nodded in agreement. 'The question is, which one?'

17

FRIDAY EARLY AFTERNOON

It was half past one before we finished taking yet more statements and establishing exactly who had been where between nine last night and nine this morning. Once again, the couples all appeared to vouch for each other, which didn't help much. Wayne the cameraman had been with Val and a few others by the campfire from eight-thirty to ten and the Pirates of the Caribbean had been up at the observation post until the small hours, after which they claimed to have returned to the hotel. Alice had dined alone and then retired to her bed.

The timeline was that from nine until eleven the previous night, the lookout post had been manned by the Pirates of the Caribbean, but nobody else had been with them to confirm that one or both of them hadn't slipped off to murder Libby. From eleven onwards, most of the group had been up there, including Julian, and I had seen them with my own eyes. Only Isabel, Val and Libby herself had been absent. Sybil and Wilfred had then volunteered to do a long observation shift while I, along with the others, had returned to camp or, in my case, the hotel. In the early hours, Geoffrey and Crispin had taken over from the elderly couple and had manned the post until breakfast time.

This meant that there were numerous possible candidates who could have done it. Being unable to pinpoint with any accuracy the time of the attack made things even trickier, although I tended to believe that my scenario of Libby having been stopped on her way down to the hotel would have made it pretty likely that the attack had taken place between nine and nine-thirty. And the only people with a watertight alibi for that period were Wilfred and Sybil, who had been with me.

After the last of them left the tent, Carmela looked across at me. 'Hungry?'

'Funny you should say that.' Spookily, Oscar also raised his head and I swear he nodded.

'Come on, then. Let's go down to the village and hope the restaurant will still serve us.' She got up with an effort and I followed her out into the open. The early-morning cloud had dissipated completely and the sun was shining from a clear, blue sky by this time and the temperature was perfect, probably in the twenties. Deliberately raising her voice so some of the campers could overhear, Carmela turned to me and spoke, in unexpectedly comprehensible English, for the benefit of anybody who might be listening in, 'Thank you, Signor Armstrong. Can I offer you lunch to say thank you?'

I gave her a deprecating wave of the hand but allowed myself to be persuaded. By now, the crime scene had been searched and the local police had also packed up and left and I was pleased to leave as well. The mood of the ufologists was understandably grim. I had sent Sandra and Maggie back to their campervan to try to get some sleep after the shock of finding what they believed to have been a dead body, and Geoffrey and Crispin looked equally shell-shocked.

I followed the squad car containing Carmela and the sergeant down to the village. There were tables with parasols outside in the little piazza in front of the restaurant and people still eating, so we sat down and Oscar positioned himself under the table at my feet. The regular waiter came out and confirmed we were still in time for a meal, giving me a grim smile of recognition as he saw us.

'Good afternoon. We were all so sorry to hear that there's been yet more tragedy up at the camp. Signorina Winter was such a very nice lady.'

The bush telegraph here in Montaz was certainly working very efficiently but, of course, it had been his boss who had phoned the police to report Libby's disappearance. I indicated the two police officers. 'I'm helping out with a bit of interpreting. By the way, would you thank Signor Arnad for informing the police this morning. I gather he's had to use his linguistic talents yet again.'

'He's not here at the moment but I will most certainly pass on the message. We're always happy to help out. Now, what would you like to eat?'

He rattled off a verbal menu and took our orders without so much as a pad and pencil. I nodded appreciatively. It's always good to see a professional at work. He told me they had just received a fresh delivery from the fishmonger so I chose grilled prawns in a chilli-pepper sauce as a starter. It came as no surprise to hear Carmela order a plate of grilled sardines and then *spaghetti alle sardine* to follow. Today's special was *lasagne al cinghiale* and I've always been partial to a bit of wild boar so I ordered that and Fournier followed my example. After the waiter had left, Carmela glanced across at me and gave an exasperated sigh.

'So many suspects with opportunity, but so little in the way of motive.'

I nodded in agreement. The interviews had revealed little or nothing that might help in discovering who had attacked Libby and why. 'It was all a bit rushed this morning. We still need to sit down and question Wayne O'Connell, Donald Grimes and Julian Goodfellow and his lady friend about Tuesday night's murder. When we mentioned Brown, Julian looked just plain angry, while Isabel looked almost sad to hear he was dead.'

'They both knew Brown pretty well, I'm sure, and I wouldn't be surprised if one or both of them really did recognise him when he was here, even though they deny it. From what you're saying, the woman quite possibly knew him better than Goodfellow did, and her reaction to hearing of Brown's death was unexpected.'

'Seeing as she was at RADA at the same time as Brown, maybe they knew each other way back then... maybe intimately.'

She nodded. 'And who knows, maybe they were still intimate more recently? If only we could find out. We definitely need to get to the bottom of how well Isabel knew Brown.'

'I should hear back from London today with a bit more info about the company where Brown and O'Connell worked, and my journalist friend is looking into the alleged suicide linked to Brown. Here's hoping that throws up some connection with somebody here.'

The waiter appeared with a carafe of red wine and a big bottle of water. Before leaving, he added, 'Barbara's made that copy of Tuesday night's surveillance footage you requested and she'll let you have it before you finish your meal. She asks if you'd like a copy of last night's footage as well – in view of the recent tragedy.'

Carmela thanked him for providing both and then, after Fournier had filled her glass with water and his and my glasses with wine, she proposed a toast.

'Here's hoping we can solve this case as soon as possible.' She gave us both a weak smile. 'Not least because from the way the baby's been kicking today, he's keen to get out any day now and I really want to crack this case first. By the way, as I feared, there were no prints on the plastic bottle that contained the petrol and the lab's still testing that piece of wood you found, so we need a breakthrough, fast.'

It occurred to me that sitting down for a meal might sound frivolous under the circumstances but the plain fact of the matter was that all we could do for the moment was wait. Besides, after a couple of years in Italy, I was under no illusions as to how important good food can be for them – and me. I glanced down at my four legged friend. I was sure he agreed with our priorities.

Just as we were finishing the meal with cups of coffee, Carmela's phone rang and she listened intently before setting it down again and looking across the table at us.

'That was my officer at the hospital. Elizabeth Winter is still alive – much to the surprise of most of the medical staff, apparently – but she's in a coma. There's no way of knowing when or if she'll come out of it, or whether she'll be in a fit state to remember what happened and to give us the name of her attacker when she does. What they say is that from the state of the wound, they're confident she was attacked as much as twelve hours before she was found, and she lay there all night. So your theory of the attack happening as she was driving back to the hotel is looking good, Dan.'

Fournier and I expressed relief that Libby was still hanging on and he then asked the question Carmela and I had been debating earlier. 'Do we think it's the same person who killed Brown?'

Carmela answered for both of us. 'I wish we knew, but if it isn't, it's quite a coincidence.'

After lunch, the two police officers returned to Aosta with the CCTV footage for Tuesday night and the previous night. I had a quiet word in Carmela's ear before she left and she promised me she would try to find time to have a rest this afternoon. I was relieved to hear her say it. Her dedication was commendable, but she had her health and that of her baby to consider.

I went up to my room and a quick check on the laptop revealed an email from Lina back at my office in Florence asking if she could accept a big investigation for next week on my behalf. This was from a local IT company handling sensitive material who had their suspicions about one or two of their staff. I replied telling her to go ahead but to tell them I might not be able to start until Tuesday. I really wanted to crack this case before I had to leave – not least to help Carmela, who was looking thoroughly drained. It was already Friday today and I very much hoped we'd be able to find our killer or killers before next week.

There was also an email from Anna's aunt. Zia Menca had clearly done her homework on the two TV companies and, as she had already hinted, it appeared that Julian's company had a reputation for being somewhat economical with the truth. She cited three examples involving alleged alien sightings that had later proved to be inventions and told me that WKTTV was currently under investigation by the broadcasting standards watchdog. Although she said she had no direct proof, it was her impression that things were not going as well for the company as we had thought.

As for CosmosLink TV, the company where Rick Brown had worked, they appeared to be more scrupulous about their fact-checking and as a result, had an altogether more credible reputation. She repeated what we already knew about Brown being an inveterate womaniser, but she regretted that she was unable to give us any names to corroborate this.

I found a short message from Jess, my journalist friend in London, saying simply:

Might have dug up a bit of dirt. I'll know better tomorrow. x

I lay back on the bed and, after the red wine and the food, I fell asleep. I was woken an hour later when my phone started ringing. It was Paul at Scotland Yard.

'Hi, Dan, I've just had a report back from DC Mallory. The guy she spoke to at CosmosLink preferred not to be named, but what he said was interesting. As far as the company's concerned, it's very successful and all seems to be going well, but Rick Brown or Browning wasn't flavour of the month with the powers that be. There had even been talk about letting him go. Apart from having wandering hands and being hauled into Human Resources pretty much on a daily basis, there are also rumours about him making himself very unpopular by going off on extravagant trips at the company's expense for no particular reason. Mallory's contact reckoned that these trips were of the dirty weekend nature rather than true research trips. Reading between the lines, I have a feeling his murder will come as a blessed relief to the company. Not that I'm saying they're the kind of people to send a hitman over to get rid of him but, one way or another, they aren't crying themselves to sleep at the news of his death.'

I thanked him most warmly and told him about the assault on Libby. It turned out he had already had a call from his sister and I told him I had sent her and her friend, Maggie, to take a rest after the shock of finding the body. I informed him in confidence that Libby was still fighting for her life and he agreed not to say anything to Sandra until he had word from me. He asked me the same question about who might have done it, and I answered honestly that I really didn't know. It was most frustrating.

18

FRIDAY AFTERNOON

Just after four, I took Oscar for a long walk, partly for his benefit and partly to clear my head and give me time to think. We found a good track leading upwards roughly in the direction of the camp and from time to time, the trees gave way to fields. From these open spaces, I had a good view up to the top of Mont Saint Georges. It was a fine afternoon and even without binoculars, I was able to pick out the tiny figures of Don and Brian, the Pirates of the Caribbean, with the sun reflecting off their silver jumpsuits as they sat by the cairn at the observation post. I took a good look around but saw nobody else in the area and no trace of alien life in the sky. It was interesting that the extra-terrestrial visitors had only made their appearance well after night had fallen and cynically, I questioned whether this might be so as to conceal their far more terrestrial origins. A phone call from Sergeant Fournier a bit later added weight to my hypothesis.

'We've been through the footage from the two hotel surveillance cameras in reception and outside the front entrance. On Tuesday night, when Brown was killed, Alice Turner's story of a drink in the bar followed by dinner appears correct and she didn't leave the hotel after that. Elizabeth Winter came back at five-thirty and her car was parked outside all night so I reckon she's in the clear as well. The two guys with the tattoos and the plaits claimed to have been on UFO duty from six o'clock that night and the tape shows them returning to the hotel at a quarter to two in the morning as they said.'

'Brown was last seen alive around five-thirty so it looks like there's no reason to suspect any of them of Brown's murder.'

'Correct. As for last night's footage, there's no sign of Elizabeth Winter but we now know she was lying unconscious in the woods. There are shots of Alice Turner on her way into the dining room at eight and coming out again at just before ten, so she's in the clear. Donald Grimes and his pal were out all evening and came back once again at almost two, but the interesting thing was that at just after midnight on both nights, three other people did leave the hotel. Two of them can clearly be seen setting off down the hill, one in a Fiat Panda and one on a scooter. I recognised the tall waiter who served us today as one of them and the other was probably the chef, going home at the end of their shift, but the third man headed *uphill* both times and didn't return for over an hour. Want to take a guess as to who that was?'

I already had a good idea who that might be. 'How about the landlord, Luigi Arnad?'

'Precisely. It was indeed Arnad. I checked his face against his photos on the hotel website and it's definitely him. The video clearly shows him disappearing up the road in his rather smart Alfa Romeo Giulia. Maybe he was making a very quick visit to a girlfriend, but, alternatively, isn't that around the time that the UFOs appear each night?'

'Exactly. If I were a betting man, I'd stake a fair amount on him being the owner of a drone or similar with a light fixed beneath it. I reckon you're right and he was out doing a bit of do-it-yourself UFO flying.'

'Our feeling entirely. He can't have been involved in the murder because he was working at the hotel on Tuesday night when Brown was killed, but the timings of his midnight sorties tie in exactly with your UFO sighting last night.' I heard him chuckle. 'I've spoken to *Commissario* Gressan – the inspector's gone home for a rest – and he doesn't think we can accuse him of anything illegal but he thinks it might be a good idea to let Arnad know that we know. It may be a bit of opportunistic business practice, but we don't like the thought of him tricking people.'

'I was thinking of having dinner in the restaurant again tonight so I can have a word if you like.'

'Do that, please. Oh, and while I remember, still no prints yet from that piece of timber but the lab says there's still hope. I'll keep you posted.'

After he had rung off, I carried on up the hill with Oscar and soon Il Convento came into view. I stopped for a drink and ended up having a cool beer in the evening sunshine and chatting with the priest, who introduced himself to me as Don Piero. He came and joined me at my table and tried prodding me for more information on the murder investigation but I pleaded ignorance and he took the hint. Instead, we chatted about everything from football – which was clearly his specialist subject – to local food and drink. He confirmed my assertion that the food down at the hotel was very good but the expression on his face when he spoke about the owner added weight to the initial impression the man had made on me.

'Luigi's not a patch on his father. Old Tommaso was a truly good man and he helped me immensely when we were first getting set up here. Luigi, I'm afraid, is far more interested in Luigi than he is in helping others.'

I made a non-committal noise and prompted him some more. 'What's his background? Has he always worked at the hotel?'

'No, he spent almost twenty years working somewhere down south. I have no idea what he was doing but he managed to make himself a load of money. Since coming back, he's spent thousands on modernising the hotel and bought himself a very nice car and every time I see him, he's wearing a different set of clothes.'

'Tell me, Don Piero, have you seen any of the UFOs that people have been talking about?'

His face split into a grin. 'I stand outside the door here every night before going to bed and look up at the heavens, but I'm thanking our Lord for granting me another day on Earth and not looking for lights in the sky. I know you're up at the camp as well but you strike me as a sensible man. Do you really believe in alien life?'

Today was Friday and I was going home on Monday at the latest, so I thought it reasonable to tell him a version of the truth. 'To be quite honest, I'm not a great believer in such things. I came here out of interest and because the universe is so huge that it's probably not wise to discount the possibility of life existing else-where, but I'm extremely dubious about these lights in the sky. In fact, I was wondering whether all this UFO activity might be contributing to the success of the hotel down there, or am I being too cynical? What do you think?'

He smiled at me again and winked. 'If I were you, I think I would ask Luigi Arnad that very same question.'

I smiled back. 'That's exactly what I intend to do this evening.'

As Oscar and I walked back down to the hotel in the twilight, I found myself thinking about Luigi Arnad and what he might have been doing before coming here. Given that he was one of the people living closest to Tuesday's murder or last night's attack on Libby, it probably made sense to get him checked out. If he had made his money by dubious means then maybe there might be a link – however unlikely – to people who would be prepared to commit murder for whatever reason. I pulled out my phone to call Carmela but then decided it could wait until tomorrow. The last thing I wanted to do was to disturb her if she was having a well-earned rest.

After a shower and a change of clothing, I gave Oscar his food and then we went down to the restaurant. When I got there, I found Alice at a table by herself and she waved me over when she saw me. Recognising her, Oscar charged across the room to greet her and let her make a fuss of him. I followed behind my dog but she didn't offer to make a fuss of me, which was probably just as well.

'Hi, Dan. Do come and join me. It'll be good to have some company.' She was still looking shell-shocked.

'Thanks a lot.' I sat down opposite her and gave her an encouraging smile. 'How're you doing? You knew Libby quite well, didn't you?'

'Not that well, really. I chatted to her a bit, but I liked her. Who would do such a thing?' She gave me a searching look.

'I don't know. The police are struggling to find a motive.' I decided to change the subject and looked around. 'Where are your pirate friends this evening?'

'On observation duty and I'm sure they'll stay on up there for tonight's light show. And let's face it, we both know that it's just a show, don't we?'

I gave a non-committal shrug. 'Who knows?'

Seconds later, the tall waiter arrived with a place setting for me and as soon as he had deposited the menu in front of me and left, Alice picked up her bottle of red and filled my glass, effectively emptying the bottle. Like the last time we had dined together, she was demonstrating that she had the same voracious appetite for alcohol that I had noticed in many other journalists. Presumably, it was the job. Mind you, I had known far too many of my colleagues in the Met with a similar propensity for alcoholic overindulgence, so I was a fine one to talk.

She picked up her glass and clinked it against mine. 'Here, Dan, we both probably need this after a day like today. But coming back to Libby's and Rick's deaths, it's bizarre to have two murders in short succession, isn't it? Do you think they were both done by the same person?'

I accepted the wine willingly but did my best to deflect her questions. She was good at her job but so was I after many years of practice dealing with media people and I managed to bat away anything too intrusive. Finally, she got the message and relented. 'So, tell me about life here in Italy. What did you do before you lived here and what made you come here?'

I decided to keep my personal affairs to myself and just told her about my writing career, but it wasn't long before she demonstrated that she really was a good investigative journalist. She caught my eye and smiled broadly.

'It's funny, I distinctly remember an inspector, sorry, chief inspector, in the Met who was called Dan Armstrong. Sound familiar to you?'

I made a vain attempt at dissimulation. 'You'd be surprised how many Armstrongs there are in Britain.'

She was still smiling as she picked up her phone and held it out towards me. 'Funny how similar you look to this handsome chap. As I remember, he was a very good detective.'

The photo on the screen was unmistakably of me that time I had had to give a statement to the media about the disappearance of a Saudi princess. As Sun Tzu probably said, every now and then in battle, there comes a moment when you have to accept defeat gracefully, so I gave her a little grin.

'Full marks, you got me. Go to the top of the class.' I let my face assume a more serious air. 'Now that you know, what are you going to do about it?'

'That's what I wanted to ask you. Would you mind if I mention your name in my next piece to my editor? I promise I wouldn't say anything bad about you.'

Although I knew from experience that promises from journalists often meant very little, I felt that I might be able to believe her, but exposing my presence here risked causing complications.

'I'd rather you didn't. I couldn't care less for my own sake, but the fact is that although I'm retired and only here because of my interest in UFOs, it could stir up a diplomatic hornets' nest. I'm sure you understand.'

I wondered how much she was buying my claim to be a keen ufologist but she nodded. 'I do. I can imagine the headlines in the Italian press – *British Police Interfere in Italian Affairs*. If the roles were reversed, I'm sure my editor would run a banner headline saying *Inspector Montalbano Shows Scotland Yard How It's Done* or some such. All right, I promise I'll leave you out of it but on one condition.'

I had a feeling I already knew what her condition would be, but I let her say it anyway. 'Go on.'

'You keep me informed on the progress of the investigations. You and I both know that we feel the same way about little green men, even if you're trying to convince people of the opposite.' She waved away my half-hearted attempt to deny it. 'It's all bullshit. We both know that. So just tell me, why are you here?'

I decided to give her a partial version of the truth. 'All right, you got me again. As far as my interest in alien life's concerned, I'm a fraud. I'm here because I'm just doing a favour to a friend by keeping an eye on his sister who's here. Initially, the idea was for me to come and offer to act as interpreter but then it seemed like a good idea for me to infiltrate the group. That's the reason I'm here pretending to be a committed ufologist, but please keep it to yourself.'

She nodded a few times and I felt reasonably reassured. After another sip of wine, she came back to her earlier question.

'So what's new in the investigation? Do you think the two deaths are connected in some way? Surely they have to be.'

'I honestly don't know, but it's likely. Let's face it, it would be a hell of a coincidence if her death wasn't linked to the first one. I can't see Libby as a murderer so it's hard to imagine that her assault was a revenge attack, but maybe she happened to see something on Tuesday night that she shouldn't have. The problem the inspector's got at the moment is putting all the pieces together. We're waiting for a few more background checks from the UK in the hope that something jumps out at us. By the way, you'll be happy to hear that I was already given your identity yesterday before you broke the news to me, so your fame preceded you.'

For the first time, the smile left her face and an expression of concern appeared in its place. 'You will keep my secret, won't you? I won't tell anybody who you are and why you're here if you do the same for me.'

'Like I told you last night, I promise I won't reveal your true identity to the people up at the camp, although of course the inspector and her men have known since yesterday that you're a journalist. I've already asked her to keep your real purpose here a secret, so don't worry. They won't give you away – and nor will I. Give me your phone number and I'll keep you in the loop.' As we exchanged numbers, I knew I wouldn't be telling her any more than I had to. Journalists – however pretty and charming – are never fully to be trusted.

At that moment, the waiter returned with my starter and I took the opportunity to order a replacement bottle of wine. As I had already had a late lunch today, I had avoided having pasta and opted for some mixed antipasti and I now found myself presented with a platter composed of salami, ham, goats' cheese on toast, roast peppers and slices of polenta topped with grilled aubergines and chopped mushrooms. It tasted as good as it looked. There was silence at the table for several minutes, punctuated only by occasional heartfelt sighs from below where my ever-hungry dog had started prodding me with his nose, indicating that he believed he was in the terminal stages of starvation. I handed down a large chunk of bread and he settled back to crunch it up and demolish it in record time. While eating, a thought came to me, and I broached the subject as soon as I had laid my fork down.

'I'm interested to know more about Libby. When I first met the two of you, and Julian was mentioned, I felt sure I saw a cloud on her face. Did she say anything to you about her relations with him? It now seems clear that the first victim was a serial womaniser and I wondered if you think maybe Julian is the same sort and she was being sexually harassed by her boss. Did she say anything to you?'

I saw her ponder the question. 'I don't remember anything in particular. I know what you mean, though. There was definitely something about Julian that was troubling her, but she never said anything to me.' She looked up, wide-eyed. 'Do you think he might have killed her to shut her up?'

'Don't go getting ideas and don't, whatever you do, mention that to your editor or both of us could be in hot water.' I caught her eye and held it. 'I mean that, Alice, not a word, promise?'

'I promise, but I'll do a bit of snooping. You never know, somebody up there may know something that they aren't prepared to tell the police. By the way, I don't think relations between Wayne and Julian are that great.'

'Has Wayne said anything? We're interviewing him tomorrow so anything you've heard would help.'

'This is only supposition at this stage, but have you seen how broken up he is today after the news of poor Libby's death?'

'Yes indeed. Do you think there was something going on between them? Or maybe he would have liked there to be?'

'I don't know, but I'll do a bit of sniffing around. He might have a guilty secret.' She looked up. 'By the way, I was sorry to read about you getting divorced. That must have been tough.'

I blinked. She really was good at sniffing about – almost as good as my canine companion – and she was clearly keen to demonstrate the extent to which she had investigated me. 'Yes, it wasn't a happy time but I'm over it now.' I avoided mentioning Anna and decided that it would be a good idea to switch the conversation from me to her. 'What about you? Married?'

Her face darkened. 'I was, but he was killed in an accident.'

'That's even tougher. I'm sorry to hear that. What happened?'

'He was knocked off his bike on his way into work just before Christmas. There was a bus behind him.' There was a catch in her voice. 'They said it must have been instantaneous.' She took another big swig of wine and I wondered whether there was a connection between her wine intake and her clearly still very raw emotions. Five or six months wasn't a very long time when it came to grieving.

'I'm so sorry. How terrible for you... and for him.' As I was speaking, I spotted the owner, Luigi Arnad, doing the rounds of the tables, schmoozing the customers. I shot Alice a glance. 'You'll have to forgive me for a few moments, but there's something I have to do when mine host comes across to talk.'

A couple of minutes later, Arnad reached our table and set about collecting our plates and checking we had enjoyed our food. As he did so, I addressed him in Italian. 'Signor Arnad, thank you for letting the inspector view the CCTV footage for the last few nights.' He looked surprised so I explained. 'One of your staff gave her a copy. The inspector asked me to ask you if you regularly go for a drive up the hill at midnight.' I caught his eye. 'Do you?'

'Sometimes.' He sounded flustered but I saw him make a stab at a bit of improvisation. 'It's nice to get out into the fresh air after an evening here in the restaurant.'

'Of course. Tell me, Signor Arnad, do you by any chance own a drone?'

An expression of horror appeared on his face but he still continued to bluster. I caught Alice looking puzzled, no doubt wondering what we were saying, and I gave her a surreptitious wink. I would give her a translation afterwards. 'A what? A drone? What would I want a drone for?'

I noted that he hadn't denied it. 'So if the inspector were to ask you to open the boot of your very nice Alfa out there, you're sure she wouldn't find anything of interest inside?'

'In my car... No, of course not...' I was sure even Oscar could hear the insincerity in his tone.

'The inspector told me to tell you she doesn't think you've been doing anything illegal, but she thought you might like to know that she takes a dim view of people who try to trick other people.'

For a moment, he looked as though he was going to continue to prevaricate but then his shoulders slumped. 'Yes, yes, of course. I see.' An air of resignation had entered his voice now.

'Good, we understand each other. So if you can think of anybody with a drone, you might like to tell them to put it back in its box and leave it there. Is that clear, Signor Arnad? I need to report back to the inspector, you see. Can I tell her it won't happen again?'

'It won't happen again.' He dropped his eyes in acceptance and I decided to capitalise on his submissive demeanour.

'Very good, the inspector will be so pleased. Now, changing the subject, can you tell me anything more about the man, Richard

Brown, who was killed on Tuesday night? He was staying here, wasn't he?'

Obviously keen to redeem himself, he frowned as he made a visible effort to concentrate. 'He was only here for one night before his death and I didn't see much of him. There was one thing, though. Our receptionist, Barbara, had a quiet word with me about the very obvious way he looked at her and some of the things he said to her that evening. She's a pretty girl, but she's very serious and hard-working and he made some indecent proposals. She said he made her skin creep.'

There was nothing surprising here, but something else occurred to me and I glanced back up at Arnad. 'Did he have any visitors while he was here?'

'I don't think so but I'll go and check with Barbara on reception.'

Picking up the plates, he hurried off and I looked across at Alice, who was quick to query what had just transpired.

'That sounded intense, Dan. Feel like giving me a translation?'

I gave her a brief summary of the conversation and she produced a wry smile in return. I was pleased to see that the pain at the memory of losing her husband appeared to have diminished – at least on the surface. She shook her head slowly.

'I've always said most of this UFO stuff was delusional rubbish – or a hoax. This just proves it. Are you going to break the news to the others that they've been had, and it was all down to a crooked hotelier?'

I had been thinking about this and I shook my head. 'Technically, we have no proof it was Mr Arnad, so the police said they were just going to let it slide. After all, our friends up at the camp aren't doing anybody any harm, so we'll let them believe what they want. They've had enough blows for one holiday.'

'I suppose you're right. And I heard you ask him about Rick Brown. Did the owner have any useful information?'

'Just that he propositioned the receptionist.'

'What a slimeball!' She gave a little shudder and for a moment, there was real hatred on her face. 'The more I hear about him, the more he repulses me. I can't say I'm sorry he's no longer with us.'

I wondered if she was referring to him no longer staying at the hotel or to his death. Either way, it was clear she didn't like the man and I shared her low opinion of him. 'Quite patently he wasn't a very nice man. As for Signor Arnad, I have to admit that this is the first time I've come across somebody trying to impersonate an alien spacecraft.'

'Well, although I couldn't hear what you were saying, I think he definitely got the message. The expression on his face was priceless. Somehow, I get the feeling his drone isn't going to get much use from now on.'

'Let's hope business continues to be good for him without it. It's a good hotel and the food's excellent, even if the UFOs aren't real.'

We both had grilled lamb chops as a main course. These were served with a mountain of little roast potatoes flavoured with rosemary and we ate the meat with our fingers. Unfortunately, the waiter who brought the food also brought the information that none of the staff could remember Richard Brown receiving any visitors or calls. I thanked him and settled down to my food. It had been an outside chance.

Followed by a couple of scoops of banana and dark chocolate ice cream, it was another excellent meal and I could feel my belt straining. Alice was looking quite weary but a bit less stressed by the time I collected the leftover scraps of lamb for Oscar and bade her goodnight.

19

SATURDAY EARLY MORNING

I didn't bother going up to the observation post on Friday night – I felt sure that there would be no lights in the sky after my talk to Arnad – and I got a most welcome good night's sleep. I was woken early by a cold, wet nose poking my shoulder, but at least this time, Oscar had stayed in his bed all night. I got up and took him for his morning walk before settling down to breakfast in the dining room. There was no sign of Alice this morning and hopefully, she had also managed to sleep well. At least I now had a better idea of why she was hitting the bottle so hard. Losing her husband like that must have been a mighty blow.

When I drove up to the camp, it was to find the fire already blazing and Val hard at work with a frying pan. The sound and smell of sizzling bacon had a magnetic effect on my dog and almost had *me* salivating before I managed to find the resolve to accept just a mug of tea from her. Oscar, on the other hand, managed to bag himself several bits of bacon rind, which disappeared down his throat in the blink of an eye. As I sipped my tea, I looked around and was pleased to see Sandra and Maggie up and about and looking less dazed than the previous day. I asked the other ufologists if they had had any luck the previous night and pretended to look surprised and disappointed when Millie told me they had seen no signs of extra-terrestrial activity.

I was just finishing my tea when I saw Julian emerge from his campervan looking immaculate as usual. Moments later, he was followed by Isabel, who was equally smart in a stylish, tailored blouse that hugged her figure. Compared to the unkempt and unwashed appearance of most of the others, they could have just stepped off a film set, make-up and all. Considering that there had been two violent assaults very close by in the past four days, they appeared remarkably unaffected. I wondered how they were going to react later on when the inspector arrived and we put them on the spot with questions about his relations with Libby, and Isabel's relations with Rick Browning.

The Pirates of the Caribbean were absent from the campfire but, after yet another late night, they were most probably sleeping it off as well. Geoffrey and Crispin were looking chirpy and appeared to have recovered from the shock of seeing what they believed to be Libby's dead body. I spared a thought for her, wondering how she was and hoping she would pull through without serious brain injury.

I didn't have time to dwell on this as my phone started ringing and I saw that it was Carmela.

'*Ciao*, Dan. We're just coming up the valley and I have some news. Feel like some breakfast? Meet at Il Convento in twenty minutes or so?'

That suited me fine and I swallowed the last of my tea and jumped to my feet, dragging a reluctant Oscar away from all the enticing smells.

I had a feeling people were going to start putting two and two together, especially when they would see Carmela return in a short while closely followed by me to interview Julian and Isabel, but by now, I couldn't care less. What was more important was to find out who our murderer (or murderers) were.

Oscar and I bounded down the slope and got to the convent before Carmela. I sat down at my usual table outside under the bamboo-covered pergola and Oscar stretched out in the shade beneath the table, panting like a steam train – in fairness, he had run twice as far as I had with all his zigzagging into the woods to find and retrieve the sticks I lobbed for him.

It was another beautiful morning and the sun was shining brightly, the snow-capped mountains almost dazzling in the light. Against the wall of the old monastery, one of Don Piero's 'guests' was making a very good job of repointing the old stone walls around two flower beds while another man was finishing planting lavender and rose bushes in them. Many of the plants going into the beds were already in flower, providing a spectacular display for the eyes and the nose. I breathed deeply and sat back, stretching my legs as I did so.

Three or four minutes later, the blue and white police car appeared and as it pulled into the car park, the two workmen melted away as if by magic. I could understand their caution and I felt a twinge of pity for them.

Carmela had dark rings under her eyes and she was looking very weary. I exchanged glances with Sergeant Fournier as they approached and he gave me a grim shake of the head. Clearly, he shared my feeling that she should be home and resting. They sat down at my table and a minute later, Don Piero himself came out to take our order. I saw his eyes flick across from me to the two police officers, but he made no comment.

I had already had a good breakfast so I just ordered a cappuccino while the other two asked for some croissants as well. After the old priest had gone off, I gave Carmela a little smile.

'And how's the mother-to-be feeling today?'

'The mother-to-be is feeling exhausted. I couldn't sleep a wink last night. So what did I end up doing? I went downstairs to the kitchen and found myself eating a tin of sardines, thinking about the case. By the way, the word from the hospital this morning is that Elizabeth is still holding on. She had a good night and her vitals are stable. The medics say they're cautiously optimistic.'

At that moment, my phone started ringing. It was Paul at Scotland Yard.

'Hi, Dan, how's the woman who got assaulted yesterday?'

'She's in a coma but she's still breathing and maybe improving a bit but news that she's still alive remains classified.'

'Great. I've got a bit more information for you. DC Mallory's friend at CosmosLink has a good friend who works at Julian Goodfellow's company, WKTTV, and he called her last night with a bit of fresh gossip. The word is that the current presenter, a lady called Isabel Sanchez, is going to be replaced any day now by a younger version. What's the name of your latest victim?'

'Libby... Elizabeth Winter.'

'Bingo. That's the one.'

This really was interesting. Did this mean that things were finally falling into place? All the same, I did my best not to get too excited as there was just one problem. 'Terrific, Paul, thanks, but I'm puzzled. If Libby knew Julian was giving her Isabel's job, why did I get the impression when I first met her that she and Julian Goodfellow didn't get on – or at least that she didn't get on with him?'

'This is only a guess, but might we be talking the proverbial casting couch? Might she have been offered the job as long as he got something in return? It wouldn't be the first time...'

'I wonder. Thanks as always, Paul. By the way, I saw Sandra half an hour ago and she's looking fine again after her shock.'

'That's good to hear. Hang on, I knew I was forgetting something. I've done a bit of digging and it turns out that her friend Maggie is a qualified accountant and she works at tvxUK as Head of Payroll and Accounts. I doubt if that involves taking her clothes off, so if you were thinking of blackmail or anything like that, it seems improbable.'

When I relayed all this information to Carmela, she looked pleased, particularly with the news about Libby taking over from Isabel. 'Well, I think that gives us a real motive for the assault on Elizabeth Winter, doesn't it? Isabel gets wind of the fact that Julian is about to replace her with the younger woman and she decides to get rid of the competition.'

'That's a pretty radical reaction.' Fournier said it before I did. He didn't look convinced and I mulled it over.

'It certainly is, but what if Isabel Sanchez not only heard that Libby was getting her job but she also discovered that Libby had been having an affair with Julian? Isabel realised she was about to lose out twice, and I can imagine that might have pushed her over the edge.'

Carmela nodded. 'You might well be right. Isabel certainly looks like a tough sort of character. Talking of tough characters, we need to have a proper talk to Donald Grimes. Although there's still no discernible motive for him to have assaulted either of the victims, his criminal record is for violence so we need to sweat him. By the way, the hospital told us that they removed pieces of bark from Libby's head wound, so that makes it pretty clear that the weapon used for the attempted murder was almost certainly a hefty lump of wood.' She looked up helplessly. 'Finding that in the middle of a forest will be like looking for a needle in a haystack.' She glanced down at the Labrador, who had rested his head on her knee and was gazing lovingly up at her. 'I don't suppose Oscar's any good as a bloodhound, is he?'

'If we were looking for something edible, maybe, but, like you say, there's a lot of wood in this forest. Having said that, he does have his moments but, like I say, identifying a chunk of wood around here is pushing it.'

'Talking of bit of wood, we've had a bit of good news.' Carmela was sounding more upbeat. 'On the way here this morning, I took a call from our forensic people and they confirm that they managed to get prints off that piece of wood that you located. As you and I thought, no surprise that they belong to Julian Goodfellow.'

This definitely came as no surprise. 'That's excellent news. We now know that he scratched the phoney impressions in the soil to make it look as though Brown's death had been the work of an extra-terrestrial vehicle.' I thought I'd better sound a note of caution. 'But that doesn't give us conclusive proof that he killed Brown. Nothing that would stand up in court.'

Carmela nodded. 'You're right, of course, but maybe if we hit him with the news that we've found his prints, he might cave and admit the whole thing.'

I wasn't convinced but I saw Fournier rub his hands together enthusiastically. 'So it could be we have a pair of murderers on our hands. Maybe he and Isabel committed both assaults together.'

20

SATURDAY MORNING

After Carmela and Fournier had left, I went into the convent shop to buy a box of biscuits as a little present for Val to thank her for all the cups of tea she'd been giving me. Don Piero was in there and I could tell he was dying to ask me how it was I'd been break-fasting with the police for the second day in a row, but he controlled himself and I didn't offer. By the time I came out with the biscuits, I was pleased to see that the two workmen had reap-peared now that the police had gone and were hard at work once more.

I met up with Carmela and Fournier back at the camp and she told me she planned to interview Julian and Isabel first, followed by Don Grimes and finally Wayne, the cameraman. We all agreed that Sandra's friend, Maggie, was no longer a person of interest.

The interview with Julian and Isabel took place in their swanky campervan. Carmela asked the questions while Sergeant Fournier listened in and I translated. Officer Chanoux remained outside the door to ensure no interruptions. The interior of the mobile home reminded me of a luxury yacht I had once visited in the course of a major drugs bust. There was little of the caravan about this place and everything about unashamed luxury. Julian certainly treated himself well.

Although I had arrived back up to the camp on foot, Isabel appeared to have already worked out who I was.

'Dan, are you a detective? You seem to be spending a lot of time with the police.' She and Julian were sitting side by side on a comfortable-looking couch but, to my suspicious eye, the distance between the two of them and the stiff way they were sitting indicated that maybe relations between them weren't as peachy as all that.

'I'm helping the inspector with the language.' I hesitated and then decided it probably wouldn't do any harm to add a bit of menace. 'But, seeing as you ask, I can confirm that until recently, I was a detective chief inspector in the Metropolitan police.'

I saw her shoot a triumphant glance at Julian. 'I told you so, Julian.' She looked – or, more correctly, glared – back at me again. 'So, Mr Detective, what have you discovered?' There was scorn and disdain in her tone and I felt myself bristling, but Carmela stepped in to bring the conversation back to the suspects. She started with Isabel herself and I translated for her.

'Your name is Isabel Sanchez and you are fifty-two years old?' Julian looked surprised. Maybe she had told him she was younger.

She nodded. 'I am.'

'Tell me about your time at RADA, Signora Sanchez. I believe you and Richard Brown met there.'

This unexpected question must have come as a surprise to Isabel and I was sure I saw a momentary look of apprehension on her face before a remarkably amiable and apparently sincere smile appeared on her lips. One thing was for sure: she might not have hit the big time but she was still a talented actor. 'How nice of you to remind me of that. I remember my years at RADA with great pleasure.'

'And Richard Brown? Do you remember him with pleasure?'

'I remember him.' She was back under control again so I took a chance in the hope of shaking her.

'We believe the two of you were close.' I knew nothing of the sort, but it was worth a shot and I was delighted to find that my guess had been right.

'It depends on what you mean by "close". We slept together a few times, if that's what you mean.'

While I was translating for the detectives' benefit, I kept a close eye on Julian and I distinctly saw his facial features change for a second or so at this revelation. I felt sure that this had come as news to him and, clearly, he didn't share his partner's thespian talents. I tried Isabel again.

'And did you stay in contact with Brown after you both left college?'

For a moment, it looked as though she was about to deny it, but Julian cut in to help her out.

'Isabel and I have known him on and off for a number of years now. He shared our belief in extra-terrestrial life, even if he had the morals of a tomcat.' I translated his words to Carmela and she turned her attention to Isabel.

'How long have you been interested in extra-terrestrial life, Signora Sanchez? Are you as hooked on it as Julian?'

Again, Isabel didn't bat an eyelid. 'On and off for most of my life. Probably since I first saw *Close Encounters*. I'm sure that film affected millions of people. And, of course, since meeting and working with Julian, I have no doubts at all. What about you, Dan? Are you a believer or was this all a charade?'

Carmela stepped in once more. 'I'd prefer it if you let us ask the questions, Signora Sanchez. Just to be clear, are you both telling me you didn't have particularly close relations with Richard Brown? You're sure you hadn't been seeing more of him recently?'

Isabel shook her head decisively. 'Only at occasional events, but never to talk to.' She was looking and sounding convincing, but something didn't quite ring true to me. I intercepted an exchange of glances between the two of them and I got the feeling that Julian didn't fully believe her either. And if he didn't, neither did I.

Carmela continued. 'And you, Signor Goodfellow? Did you see much of Brown?'

'As little as possible. He was a hateful man and if I had known who he was when he turned up here, I would have sent him packing.'

In the meantime, Isabel had decided to go on the offensive. 'Now, when are we going to be allowed to leave? You can't keep our passports indefinitely. I've decided I want to leave early, maybe as early as tomorrow.'

'Two people are dead, Signora Sanchez. Do you realise that?' Carmela's voice was icy and I did my best to reproduce her tone when I translated. 'Both of them were murdered. You will leave Montaz when I say you can leave and not before, although I'd like you to leave this *vehicle* now. I need to have a few words with Signor Goodfellow on his own, so would you be so kind as to leave us until I call you back?' She didn't give Isabel a chance to object. 'Sergeant, please escort the lady outside.'

If looks could have killed, Carmela would have been lying dead on the floor, but she completely ignored Isabel until the door had closed behind her and then she transferred her attention fully onto Julian.

'Now, Signor Goodfellow, why don't you tell me why your fingerprints are all over a piece of timber used to make a childish attempt to fool the gullible into thinking the death of Mr Brown was caused by an extra-terrestrial craft?'

The supercilious expression on Julian's face disappeared in a flash, to be replaced by a shifty look. 'Fingerprints, you say?'

'Yes, Signor Goodfellow, your fingerprints on a piece of evidence that links you very clearly with the murder of Richard Brown.'

Now there was fear on Julian's face. 'All right, Inspector, they are my prints, but I was only using the piece of wood to draw. I had nothing to do with Brown's murder, I promise.' There was a much more respectful note in his voice now. 'It was a stupid thing to do, and I bitterly regret it. I went up there and did it after your officers had left, but that's all I did, I swear. But that doesn't link me with the murder, you know. You have to believe me.'

Carmela wasn't giving up and I admired her steely resolve. 'Signor Goodfellow, exactly where were you on Tuesday evening between the hours of five and nine-fifteen?'

'I've already told you, Inspector. I was here with Isabel.'

'So the only person who can vouch for you is your partner.' She held up an admonitory hand to stop him from speaking. 'Richard Brown was killed by a blow to the head. I've been trying to work out why on earth the killer then went to the trouble of setting fire to his body. But, of course, I now see that this was deliberately done to make the event look as if it had alien origins. The fact that you don't deny going back and trying to fake the signs of a landing in the earth up there leads me to one inevitable conclusion. I put it to you, Signor Goodfellow, that you killed Richard Brown and then dreamt up this extra-terrestrial charade to cover your tracks and to add credence to your profitable little business taking money off the gullible. What do you have to say for yourself?'

Our eyes focused on Julian, who was clearly searching for words.

'I've killed nobody, not even when I was in the army. I could never do anything of the kind. Yes, I confess I went up there after the police had left and I drew those marks in the earth, but I didn't kill Browning or set fire to his body. You must believe me.' He was sounding increasingly desperate and I found myself tending to believe his denials. 'I know it was incredibly stupid, but I felt it was too good an opportunity to miss. I know what I saw in the Andes, but nobody wants to believe me.' His voice became more pathetic. 'I'd just like to be taken seriously for once.'

'And defacing a murder scene was your way of making sure you're taken seriously? Listen, Signor Goodfellow, I don't believe you. I know you're hiding something and I *will* find out the truth.' The disdain in Carmela's voice was palpable. 'And I mean the real truth, not the sort of lies you promote in your TV shows.'

Julian hung his head. 'I've told you the truth, Inspector, I really have.'

'Moving on from Tuesday night to Thursday night, what can you tell me about the murder of Libby Winter? Were you involved with that as well?'

This time, he definitely looked appalled. 'No, of course not. I liked Libby. In fact I liked her a lot.'

'When you say you liked her a lot, just how much and in what way? Were the two of you involved in a sexual relationship?'

He shook his head emphatically – but not totally convincingly. 'No, of course not. What gave you that idea?'

Carmela ignored his question. 'I understand that you were about to give her the role in the company currently occupied by your partner, Isabel. I imagine Libby was happy about that. Yes?'

He was now looking frankly stunned. 'Who on earth told you that? That's classified information.'

'There's no such thing as classified information in a murder investigation. So you're not denying that this was the plan. Answer my question please: was Libby happy to be offered the new position?'

'Well, yes, obviously she was...' Julian was flapping around like a freshly caught fish on the deck of a boat.

'And was she grateful? Or did the new job come at a price? I have witnesses who say that relations between the two of you were strained. What did you ask for in return?'

'Nothing... I asked for nothing.' I felt pretty sure even Julian himself could hear the insincerity in his voice. 'Really, nothing happened between us... nothing.'

'But you would have liked something to happen, wouldn't you?'

'No, of course not. I'm with Isabel.'

'Ah, yes, Isabel. Somehow, I don't think she can have been too happy to be replaced by a woman half her age. That must have hurt.' I kept my eyes trained on his as I added a couple of questions of my own. 'When did you break the news to Isabel that she was being replaced? On Thursday afternoon, maybe? That's what I've been told.'

I saw him hesitate, obviously considering denial, before he caved in. 'Yes, it was on Thursday afternoon. I told her then and, no, she wasn't happy.'

'Unhappy enough to go out that evening and kill the woman who was usurping her position?'

He shook his head but, again, I sensed no real conviction. 'Of course not. Isabel isn't a murderer.'

I tried another little dig of my own. 'Or did Libby maybe turn you down? And when I say turn you down, I'm referring to the job and the quid pro quo that came with it. Did she say no and did that make you angry enough to kill her?'

'Oh no, no, no. For God's sake, no. I would never have harmed her.' I tended to believe him this time, although what he said next didn't ring as true to me. 'There was no quid pro quo. What sort of man do you take me for?' Now he was blustering and I could hear it, but maybe he wasn't lying about not having tried to kill Libby. I told Carmela what I thought and as I produced the translation, she gave Julian an acid glare.

'Signor Goodfellow, what we need to discover is exactly what sort of man you are.' She turned towards the sergeant. 'Fournier, please ask Signora Sanchez to come back in and, at the same time, would you escort this gentleman outside, making sure that he and the woman don't speak to each other?'

A few seconds later, a chastened Julian's place on the couch was taken by Isabel, who looked as though she was only just managing to control her temper. Before Carmela could make a start on the questions, Isabel launched an attack.

'Well, what am I accused of? Do you think I killed both of them, or only one?'

She was so nearly snarling that Oscar, who in his usual friendly way had been trotting across to say hello, stopped, turned around and came back to my side, looking up at me as much as to say, *What's her problem?*

Carmela replied with perfect calm and I did my best to keep my tone equally level as I translated. 'Nobody's accusing you of anything... yet, but I'm interested that you think we might consider you capable of murder. It may interest you to hear that I do.' She let that sink in for a moment or two before continuing. 'Of course, when you heard that you were losing your job to a younger, prettier woman, I imagine murder must have gone through your head.'

This did a very effective job of curbing Isabel's rising anger. Her expression of bitter antagonism was momentarily wiped from her face before the actor in her took over and she switched on a cute little girl, lost look.

'Me, Inspector? I could never murder anybody.' *Except you* was the unspoken threat.

'And you maintain that you were with Signor Goodfellow between nine o'clock and eleven o'clock on Thursday night when Elizabeth Winter was attacked?'

'I've already told you that.'

'And the two of you were together between five and nine on the night that Brown was murdered as well?'

'Absolutely, and there's no way you can prove otherwise, can you?'

Carmela ignored the question. 'Now that your current partner isn't listening, I want you to tell me the truth about you and Richard Brown.' I rather liked the way Carmela added just enough emphasis to the word 'current' to convey her scepticism about the relationship and I distinctly saw the barb hit home, but then a second or two later, Isabel's RADA training kicked in once more.

'But I already told you, Inspector, or weren't you listening? I barely knew the man. Or maybe your trained monkey doing the translating didn't translate properly.' I found myself smiling at 'trained monkey'. I thought that was a nice touch. Over my years as a detective, I had found over and over again that suspects being interviewed who felt threatened – mainly because they had something to hide – either opted for a sycophantic sweetness or outright aggression when dealing with awkward questions. The reaction of those with nothing to hide normally ended up somewhere between the two. Although I knew that this gut feeling of mine wouldn't hold up in a court of law, it reinforced my belief that Isabel Sanchez had a guilty conscience – to what extent remained to be seen.

The fact of the matter, though, was that Isabel was dead right: we didn't have any concrete proof against her for either night, and she knew it. She drew herself up and launched an all-out assault. 'If you really think I was involved in these appalling murders, then arrest me, but you'll need evidence and you haven't got any. And if you aren't going to arrest me, you need to give me back my passport and let me leave.'

Once again, she was spot on. The fact was that we had no proof of guilt of murder or attempted murder against either of them or, indeed, any of the other ufologists. I glanced across at Carmela and saw her come to a decision.

'I want you and your companions to stay in Italy until we've exhausted all lines of enquiry. Signor Goodfellow said you are planning to stay for two weeks, so stay for your second week and keep looking for flying saucers. By the end of next week, I expect to have reached a satisfactory conclusion to this case.' She waved away Isabel's attempts to protest. 'If necessary, I'll go to court and hit you with a restraining order. If you attempt to leave this area before I say so, you will be arrested. Is that clear?'

Isabel made no response but I caught a glint in her eyes that indicated that she knew she had us over a barrel. We could have all the suspicions in the world but, without proof, there was no way we could mount a successful case against her or Julian. I cast another thought to Libby, lying critically injured in a hospital bed. If only she were to regain consciousness and, with it, her memory. There was little doubt in my mind that Isabel and maybe even Julian were responsible for the attack on Libby that had so nearly killed her. And quite possibly the murder of Richard Brown as well.

21

SATURDAY MORNING

The two detectives and I left Julian and Isabel's campervan and went across to the squad car so as to be out of reach of curious ears. Carmela was looking ever more tired and drawn, and I was pleased to see Fournier chivvy her into taking a seat while he and I stood outside the open door. Meanwhile, Oscar adopted his 'I'm starving' look and wandered across to the campfire where Val was still sitting as she had been all week. Alongside her was her daughter and opposite them were Wilfred and Sybil. Alice was sitting a bit further along, chatting to the Pirates of the Caribbean. As she saw me, she gave me a little wave and I waved back but stayed out of earshot.

'Well, gentlemen, what do you think of Goodfellow and Sanchez?' Carmela cradled her bump with both hands and gave a heartfelt sigh. 'An unsavoury pair of liars or a couple of innocent victims of police harassment?'

The sergeant snorted. 'Innocent? No way. They're both as guilty as sin. Maybe both of them killed Brown and then they also tried to kill Winter, or one assaulted one and one the other, but I'm in no doubt about their guilt – particularly the woman. She's a nasty piece of work.' He glanced across at me. 'What do you think, *Commissario*?'

'You don't need to call me "*Commissario*"; it's just Dan these days. I agree with you that they're a suspicious couple, but we need proof. Both had opportunity on either night as their only alibis come from each other. Both had means – after all, the forest's littered with rocks and branches, and both are strong enough to swing one. Julian has motive as far as Brown's industrial espionage is concerned – although, let's face it, murder is a bit extreme – and Isabel had reason to want Libby out of the way. What we don't have are any witnesses who can attest to having seen either or both of them out and about. Yes, there are Julian's prints on the plank of wood he used to scratch the marks in the earth, but that won't be enough to convince a judge or jury that he also killed Brown. After all, if he did kill Brown, why didn't he set fire to the body and scratch those marks at the same time to bolster the UFO charade? No, we need more. Let's just hope that Libby comes out of her coma and tells us who assaulted her.'

Carmela nodded and glanced over towards the campfire. 'The next two suspects are Donald Grimes and Wayne O'Connell. Shall we start with Grimes, seeing as he's up here at the moment and not down at the hotel? Fournier, ask him to go into the tent and we'll join him there.' As the sergeant went off to speak to Don, Carmela beckoned me closer and lowered her voice. 'Dan, can I ask you a favour, please?'

I lowered my head towards the open door. 'Anything.'

'Don't say anything to Fournier for now, but I think I might just have felt a small contraction. The midwife said it was likely to be any day now.' Seeing the concern on my face, she wagged a finger at me. 'Not a word, all right? Anyway, what I wanted to ask you was: if I get carted off to hospital before the investigation's over, would you be prepared to step in and hold Fournier's hand? He's a good officer, but I'm sure he'd appreciate having your experience beside him. Pierre is of course officially in overall charge of the investigation but I spoke to him this morning before we came up here and he asked me to tell you it would be a great help to him. Will you be able to do that? To be honest, he didn't want me to come here at all today.'

'Of course I will. No problem. Give me Pierre's number just in case.' I waited until I had punched the number into my phone before leaning even closer to her. 'But my agreement comes with a stipulation: as soon as we finish interviewing these two men this morning, you get somebody to drive you straight back to Aosta – or I'll do it myself.' Before she could protest, I carried on. 'Pierre's right. You have one overriding responsibility at the moment and it's not to this case. Fournier's a good man and of course I'll stick with him, but you need to remember that your first responsibility is to your unborn child. Pierre said it and I'm saying it – it's time for you to go.'

'No, but...' I saw a little spasm of pain flit across her face.

'In fact, forget Don and Wayne. Fournier and I'll interview them. You need to get out of here right now.' Ignoring her weak protests, I beckoned to Officer Chanoux and he came running over. 'Chanoux, the inspector needs to get back to Aosta, maybe to the hospital, right now. Can you take her in your car while I stay here with Sergeant Fournier?'

'Yes, of course, if...' He looked down at Carmela, who finally gave in and nodded.

'It's probably for the best.' She gave me a weary smile. 'Thanks, Dan.'

Chanoux helped her out and into his police Alfa and seconds later, they were making their way down the track to the road with the blue light flashing. I called Oscar and walked across to the tent, stopping to brief the sergeant before we went in to speak to Donald Grimes.

He nodded in agreement. 'I must confess to feeling immensely relieved. The inspector's been driving herself too hard. She should have gone off last week, if not a few weeks earlier.'

I glanced towards the tent. 'You and I can interview Grimes and the cameraman and then you can report back to *Commissario* Gressan. Are you happy for me to lead or do you want to pitch the questions and I'll just translate?'

'I'd be very grateful if you would do most of the questioning, *Commiss...* Dan. If you could keep throwing me the translations, and if anything occurs to me, I'll add my own questions.' He gave me a little grin. 'Having somebody with your experience to take over makes my life a lot easier.'

I clapped him on the shoulder. 'You'd be fine on your own, I'm sure, but I'm very happy to help. Right, let's go and see what Mr Grimes has to say for himself.'

Inside the tent, Don was sitting bolt upright on one of the chairs by the trestle table with his back to the entrance. As usual, he was wearing his shiny spacesuit. He must have heard us walk in but he didn't turn around. Fournier and I took our seats opposite him and I explained what was going to happen.

'Inspector Costey has had to return to Aosta but she's asked the sergeant and me to put some questions to you. We'll be recording the interview so please ensure that you tell us the whole truth.'

To my surprise, he actually smiled. 'How does it go again? "Anything you say will be taken down and may be used against you"? Something like that. I've had it said to me enough times, you'd think I'd remember.' His expression hardened. 'I presume that's why you've singled me out but, before you start trying to pin anything on me, I need to tell you that I've changed. Yes, I used to be a bit of a tearaway, I did some stupid things, but I've grown up over the past few years.' He caught my eye. 'You'd be amazed how twenty-five months and sixteen days in prison can make a person sit down and evaluate his whole life. It worked for me. I'm just here on holiday, doing what I like doing, and I had nothing to do with what's happened.'

I translated for Fournier's benefit and while I did so, I kept my eyes on Don's face. Doing my best to ignore the bizarre hieroglyphs plastered all over it, I got the impression that he was telling the truth, but I decided to push him a bit just to be sure.

'The fact is, Don, that you have no real alibi for Tuesday night or last night, have you? Are you seriously telling me you had nothing to do with either murder?'

'Why would I want to kill a harmless little thing like Libby or some bloke dressed up all weird like the Mummy?'

Considering his own appearance, I felt he was taking a bit of a chance accusing somebody else of looking weird, but I made no comment. Instead, I had one last try. 'So you're telling me you had nothing to do with either murder?'

He looked me straight in the eye. 'Yes, I am. On my mother's life, I swear it. I'm not a killer, you've got to believe that.'

Whether it was the tone of his voice or some inexplicable canine instinct, Oscar got up from where he had been assiduously licking himself clean – not one of his more endearing habits – and trotted over to the other side of the desk, where he sat down alongside Don, resting his nose on the man's thigh. Don looked down and stroked his ears. 'Well, at least your dog believes me.'

In fact, that made two of us. Looking back over my career in the police, I could probably count on the fingers of one hand the number of times I got a suspect completely wrong. I've developed pretty good antennae when it comes to sorting out whether the person sitting in front of me is telling me the truth or lying through his teeth – although I can't claim to have got it right every time. My feeling now was that Don wasn't our murderer. I asked him a few more questions, checking up on exactly when and why he and his friend Brian had come here, until I felt satisfied he could be excluded from any further inquiries. I finished by asking him for his take on what had happened and his answer was interesting.

'You didn't hear this from me, right? I get on okay with most people and I don't want to cause trouble in the camp but, for my money, I don't like the look of Isabel. I'd never met her before, although I'd seen her on TV – you know, she does the extra-terrestrial-life programmes. On TV, she's all smiles and charm itself, but here, she's been distant and unapproachable, full of herself. Maybe she's just a cow, or maybe she and Julian are in the middle of a break-up. I don't know. Certainly, there doesn't seem to be much love lost between the two of them.' He pointed towards Oscar, who by now, job done, had slumped down onto the floor at his feet. 'You know how dogs raise their hackles and growl when they see something they don't like? Well, that's how she's been.'

'You're not the first person to mention that. What about her relations with Libby?'

'Brian and I reckon that Libby and Julian were carrying on together. There was just something about the way he looked at her. And if we could see it, then you can bet your life that Isabel noticed as well, and that would account for her being so hostile. Like I say, if I were in your shoes, I'd be trying to pin at least one of the murders on Isabel.' For a moment, he looked around almost furtively. 'But leave me out of it. I didn't tell you anything.'

After I had let him go, I talked it over with Fournier and we both agreed that Don was probably in the clear, but that the evidence – or at least the accusations – against Isabel were ramping up.

Before I could bring in our final interviewee, Fournier got a call and passed his phone across to me.

'It's *Commissario* Gressan. He wants to talk to you.'

I took the phone from him. 'Good morning, Pierre. I thought I might be hearing from you.'

'*Ciao*, Dan. I've just been talking to Carmela. I'm delighted she's finally agreed it's time to look after herself and think about having her baby. She says you put her in the car yourself, so well done. Anyway, are you sure you don't mind helping out?'

'Mind? I'm delighted to help out. Sergeant Fournier has just been interviewing the last of our main suspects now and I've been lending a hand. Is there any chance we could meet up some time today so we can talk you through the whole thing before we take any fresh steps? Would you like us to come down to Aosta?'

'Yes, let's meet up, but there's no need for you to come all the way to Aosta. I have to be in Cervinia this afternoon to see the *Carabinieri* station commander about another matter so I'll call in at the ufologists' camp first and then why don't you and Fournier come with me to Cervinia for lunch? I know a very good restaurant up there.'

'Sounds like a good idea. Apart from anything else, I haven't been up there yet and it'll be good to get a close-up look at the Matterhorn. And this time, I'm paying for lunch.'

'We can argue about who pays once we've had the meal.' From his tone, I had a feeling this was one argument I was probably going to lose. Something I love about the Italians is how generous they are, but this makes it very hard to be allowed to pay for a meal. On the occasions on which Anna and I had been out with Zia Menca, I'd had to slip off partway through to stuff a handful of banknotes into the cashier's hands to prevent her from paying.

When I told Fournier what had been agreed, he beamed. 'It'll be just like old times for me. When I was starting out, I was assigned as a constable to *Commissario* Gressan, Inspector Gressan as he was then, but then he got promoted and I got promoted. He's a good boss and he likes his food!'

I glanced down at Oscar. 'Don't we all?' A thought occurred to me. 'By the way, who has the passports? I'd quite like to take a look at who's been where and when, just in case that throws up any anomalies.'

'They're in Inspector Costey's office.' He pulled out his phone. 'I can make sure they get given to the *Commissario* to bring up here with him. Tell me, what do you mean by "anomalies"?'

'I won't really know until I look. I remember a drugs case we had a few years back where we managed to establish that the main dealer and the hitman he engaged to kill a rival had both been in Bogota on the same day. It's worth a try. Now, if you'd like to make that call and then go and find the cameraman, we need to talk to him.'

The first thing I asked Wayne O'Connell was about his previous job.

'I understand you've been working for WKTTV for six months now?'

'Yes.' He had removed his cowboy hat and I was surprised to see that he was almost completely bald beneath it. He was wearing the same expression of deep sadness he had been exhibiting ever since word of Libby's death had circulated.

'And before that, you worked for CosmosLink TV.'

'Yes.'

'Could you tell me about the circumstances under which you left that company? I understand there was some trouble.'

He looked up with consternation on his face. 'So you heard about that?' He gave a frustrated sigh. 'I was afraid of that. Now you're going to try to pin Rick Browning's death on me, aren't you?'

'We'll pin his death on you if you did it, but if you're innocent, you have nothing to fear. Tell me what happened that resulted in you being fired.'

He shook his head. 'I wasn't fired, I left. I couldn't work in the same company as that bastard any more.' This wasn't what the HR person at CosmosLink had told Paul but, for now, I made no comment.

'The way I heard it, there was talk of you assaulting Brown. Tell me what happened and, above all, tell me why it happened.'

'It was all about a girl called Sally, Sally Bowerman. She worked at the company as a researcher and Browning used to take her with him when he jetted off to investigate supposedly alien discoveries. The day after they came back from South Africa at the end of November, I found her in tears. Long story short, Browning had tried to rape her on the last night. If he hadn't been hopelessly drunk, he would have succeeded, and she had had to barricade herself in her hotel room with him pounding on the door. She wedged a chair under the doorhandle of her room and didn't sleep a wink all night. She said she was terrified.'

'Why tell *you*, Wayne? Why didn't she go to her boss or to HR?'

'That's what I told her to do, but we both knew it would be a waste of time. His sort always win. The reason she told me about it is because the two of us were friends.'

'How friendly were you? Were you close? Intimate, maybe?'

He bristled. 'Just friends. There was nothing like that going on. I'm not like Browning.'

'And is it true you assaulted him?'

'I didn't hurt him. I just grabbed him by the collar and told him what I thought of him. Sally handed in her notice and I did the same. Like I told you, I couldn't work in the same space as him.'

'And then the job at WKTTV came up and you applied for it. Did you tell Julian why you left CosmosLink? I imagine he was delighted to hear you hated Brown. What about Sally, what happened to her?'

'I'm not sure. She went back home to Dundee and I haven't heard any more from her.'

'Now tell me, at what point did you realise that the man in the bandages who turned up here on Monday was Browning?'

'I didn't know it was him, not until the boys said they'd seen it on the Internet.' My antennae were twitching this time. I couldn't put my finger on it yet but I felt sure he wasn't telling me the whole truth so I prodded him some more.

'But that's not true, is it, Wayne? You did recognise him, didn't you? Did you recognise him all by yourself or did somebody tell you who it was under the disguise?'

'Nobody told me, I didn't realise. That's the truth.' He was blustering and I felt sure he was lying, but the fact was that I had no evidence to use to contradict what he said.

'Tell me about Libby.' I remembered Carmela telling me about the video footage Wayne had shot of Libby's bottom. 'You liked her, didn't you?'

He grimaced. 'Yes, I liked her and I felt sorry for her. What is there to tell? She was a nice, sweet girl and they killed her.' It occurred to me that a beautiful young woman would have been unlikely to fall for an overweight, bald, forty-something like Wayne. Quite possibly the same had applied to the other girl, Sally. Maybe he had lusted after both women but been spurned and this unrequited love had exploded into Thursday night's violent assault.

'You say they killed her. Who's "they"?'

He looked me straight in the eye. 'Isabel and Julian, of course.'

'Have you any proof to back up that allegation?'

'Proof, no, but I'm sure of it. Julian told her he would give her Isabel's job, but only if she slept with him.'

'She told you that?'

'Well, no, but it was pretty obvious.' He caught my eye again. 'To me at least. When Isabel found out she was being replaced, she must have been very bitter. Either Julian killed her to keep her from telling people he'd propositioned her, or Isabel killed her out of spite. Take your pick, either of them could have done it.'

I couldn't fault his deductions. They were exactly the same as my own. 'But you have no proof?'

He just shook his head.

22

SATURDAY AFTERNOON

Lunch with Pierre Gressan and Sergeant Fournier was predictably good, although Cervinia was less attractive than I had been expecting. Unlike Zermatt, its quaint, traditional, Swiss counterpart on the other side of the Matterhorn, Cervinia was a predominantly twentieth-century conglomeration of holiday apartments, ski-hire shops, hotels, bars and restaurants. To my taste, there was more Alpine atmosphere in the little village of Montaz with its old stone houses and tiny church, although in Cervinia, there was no escaping the stunning backdrop of the mountains. The town stood at the head of the valley at over two thousand metres and the barren landscape of the surrounding slopes was testament to the fact that for half of the year, much of it was usually buried beneath a layer of snow, even if this year, according to the barman in Valtournenche, had been exceptionally warm.

Immediately beyond the last buildings, the mountainside started to rise steeply and it just kept on climbing ever more sharply towards the rocky pinnacle of the Matterhorn at almost four and a half thousand metres of elevation. A few wisps of cloud were forming right up at the top of the mountain and by the end of the meal, it had been completely masked from our view. Pierre told me that this meant we could expect rain later, although the rest of the sky was still cloudless. I bowed to his superior local knowledge and made a note to dig out a waterproof just in case.

The restaurant chosen by Pierre occupied the ground floor of a bland-looking apartment block, but the view from the plate-glass windows was spectacular. We looked out onto the cables of the main cable car linking Cervinia with the glacier on top of the Monte Rosa where people can ski all year round. The massive wall of rock appeared to be bearing down on us and the sensation was almost intimidating – not that it bothered Oscar, whose olfactory senses had gone into overdrive as we had walked in. He stationed himself at my feet, his attention trained on the table, nostrils flared. It was almost as if he were begging me to pass him down the menu so he could choose – although, knowing him, he would just have chosen everything.

After a starter of hand-carved, cured ham and, inevitably, pieces of Fontina and other different cheeses, we all chose roast venison served with tiny little roast potatoes and an assortment of grilled vegetables. As we ate, we discussed the case. Pierre listened intently until Fournier and I had brought him up to speed before he set down his fork and summed it all up.

'Let's start with the easy one. It sounds to me very much as though the attempted murder of Elizabeth Winter has to have been committed by either Julian Goodfellow or his lady friend, Isabel Sanchez. Do you both agree with that?'

I answered this time. 'Yes, and we both feel that it's more likely the work of the woman than the man. Isabel Sanchez was informed by Julian only a few hours before the assault that she was going to be replaced by Libby. If Wayne O'Connell is right about Julian Goodfellow having an affair with Libby, then that gives us two reasons why Isabel Sanchez might have done it.'

'Fine. As for the murder of Richard Brown, Julian Goodfellow still looks like the most likely candidate for that one as well, but the problem we have for both of these cases is that there appears to be no definitive proof of any kind. Yes, you have proof that Goodfellow went back to the scene after my officers had finished and the corpse had been removed, in order to scratch some marks in the ground to further his UFO cause, but there's no way a judge would see that as proof of murder.' He reached for his glass of red and took a sip before continuing. 'We need proof and we need it in the next seven days or there's no way we'll be able to keep our suspects here. Do we all agree that that's the situation?'

Fournier and I nodded again.

Pierre returned to his food, his brain no doubt churning as ours were doing. Just then, my phone started ringing and I saw that it was Jess, my journalist friend in London.

'Hi, Jess, what have you got for me?'

'Hi, Dan, apologies for the delay but I had a sick child on my hands yesterday. I managed to dig up the suicide story and although nothing was ever proved and it never got as far as a police investigation, it seems pretty clear that the woman who killed herself did so out of love for Richard Brown, or Browning as he was known. Her name was Tracey Burgess and she lived in Brixton. She and Brown had been carrying on a liaison for over a year before he dumped her earlier this year for a younger woman. She freaked out and took an overdose at the end of January. In the note she left behind, she blamed Brown by name but as he hadn't done anything illegal – morally reprehensible, yes– it all died a death, just like she did, poor thing.'

I had been scribbling in my notebook as she was talking. 'Tracey Burgess, thanks. I'll do a bit of checking this end. Thanks a lot for your help, Jess.'

'Any time. So, do you think you'll crack the case? When you do, you will remember me, won't you? A nice exclusive would be most welcome.'

'I'll certainly keep you informed about developments, but I can't promise an exclusive. The *Mirror* have already sent one of their people, a woman called Alice Turner, and she's been feeding them exclusive stories.'

'Oh, well, better luck next time for me. Here's wishing you luck with the case. Bye, Dan.'

I recounted what Jess had told me to my two companions and Fournier and I ran through the surnames of the ufologists without finding anybody called Burgess, so it seemed unlikely that the woman had been related to anybody here. Pierre handed me the passports of the group and I flicked through those as well, checking the female members' maiden names where applicable. Still no Burgess. The next thing to check would be whether the woman had been known to any of the group or whether she had maybe worked with, or had even gone out with, any of them. Our deliberations were interrupted by a call to Pierre. After a brief conversation, he put down the phone and told us the news.

'That was the hospital. Elizabeth Winter has woken from her coma and she's talking. One of the doctors there studied in the UK and speaks good English. He tells us she has positively identified the person who tried to kill her. She says her assailant was waiting at the side of the road with a story about showing her an alien arte-fact hidden in the bushes.' He looked at us both with a sparkle in his eye. 'Feel like making a suggestion?'

Fournier and I answered in unison. 'Isabel Sanchez.'

'Dead right.' There was real satisfaction in Pierre's voice. 'Now, I heartily recommend the home-made panna cotta they do here. After that, I think we have an appointment with Signora Sanchez, don't you?' He picked up his glass and held it out towards us. 'A toast to Elizabeth Winter. Here's hoping she makes a full and speedy recovery.'

Fournier and I drank to that and I couldn't help a little smile. Although we now had proof that Isabel Sanchez was at the very least guilty of attempted murder, this wasn't going to interfere with Commissario Gressan's enjoyment of his lunch. I felt sure Oscar approved.

We got back up to the camp at just after two-thirty and found most of the group sitting around the fire looking downhearted. As far as I could see, all of them were there apart from Julian and Isabel. Val told me that after they had seen no sign of alien life the previous night, this morning had proved equally barren, and I could sense the growing frustration. The fact that the sky was beginning to cloud over as predicted by Pierre probably didn't help to improve the mood either. Crispin and Geoffrey told us they had just been replaced up at the observation post by Julian and Isabel, so Pierre, Fournier and I set off up the track to speak to the two of them.

Oscar trotted happily ahead of us, as usual looking out for sticks to retrieve. The wind was picking up now and, although it was far from cold, the temperature among the trees was noticeably lower than it had been at the camp. By the time we got up to the cairn on the summit, the sun had disappeared and the wind was strong enough to buffet us as we made our way along to the two figures sheltering in the lee of a boulder. When Julian spotted us, he got to his feet, but Isabel remained sitting. As agreed, I did the talking.

'Isabel Sanchez, these officers have come to arrest you for the attempted murder of Elizabeth Winter. Stand up, please.'

Isabel stayed where she was. 'I'm quite comfortable here, thank you. Please stop playing games and leave me in peace, you annoying little man. You have no proof against me so, until you do, I'd be grateful if you would leave me alone.'

I had been expecting no less from her so I pointed to my companions. 'Isabel, you've met Sergeant Fournier before and this is *Commissario* Gressan of the Aosta police and he has some news for you.'

All eyes turned to Pierre and I translated as he started speaking. 'I've just had a telephone call from the hospital to inform me that the woman you tried to kill so brutally has emerged from her coma.' Julian's jaw actually dropped in surprise, but I couldn't miss the flicker of fear that passed across Isabel's face. 'Elizabeth Winter told us you flagged her down with a story of showing her an alien artefact. You lured her out of her car and into the bushes, where you assaulted her. Sound familiar? That's all the proof we need. Now will you stand up or do I need to ask my sergeant to grab you by the scruff of the neck and haul you to your feet? I'm quite prepared to lead you back down this mountain with your arms handcuffed behind your back if you don't cooperate. If you trip and fall, that's your lookout.' He let his voice harden and I did the same as I translated. 'Now stand up.'

As Isabel pulled herself grudgingly to her feet, Julian caught my eye. 'She isn't dead? Libby isn't dead? But I thought...'

'You thought Isabel had killed her, didn't you?' I took a step towards him. 'Or were you both in on it together?'

'No, no, of course not. I didn't know anything about it.' He turned towards Isabel, his arms flapping helplessly at his sides. 'You didn't try to kill Libby, did you? I mean, you wouldn't, would you?'

Isabel subjected him to a withering sneer. 'You didn't think I'd have the guts to kill the woman who's just ruined my life? I know you haven't the guts to kill anybody, but that's the difference between you and me, Julian. You live in a world of your own invention, but I live in the real world.' She transferred her attention to Pierre. 'I'm sorry I didn't manage to kill the little bitch. If I had done, you wouldn't have been able to accuse me of anything, would you?'

Pierre completely ignored her and turned towards Julian. 'Tell me something, Signor Goodfellow, when you were questioned about the murder of Richard Brown, you told us you and this lady had spent Tuesday evening together in your caravan. Are you absolutely sure that's what happened or would you like to change your story now? After all, even she admits that she has attempted murder. It's only by a miracle that Elizabeth Winter wasn't killed by her. Think carefully, Signor Goodfellow, what did happen on Tuesday night when Richard Brown was killed?'

To our surprise, the answer was provided by Isabel, the expression on her face as she looked at her partner one of undisguised disgust. 'Go on, then, Julian, tell them what happened, or shall I? All right, I will.' She returned her attention to the rest of us. 'We were walking up the track towards the observation post when we heard a scream and a thud and then running footsteps through the trees. We went to investigate and we found the remains of the man we knew as Nick Green with his head smashed in, the bandages covering his face swamped with blood.'

'What time was this?' I kept my voice low so as not to disturb her flow.

'Six, six-thirty.' This time, it was Julian who spoke up, his voice little more than a croak. 'He was dead, there was no doubt about it. I checked for a pulse just in case, but he was dead.'

'So you deny killing him?'

Julian looked horrified and even Isabel's sneer was momentarily shaken from her lips. He answered for both of them. 'Of course we didn't kill him. We didn't even know who he was.'

'Do you really expect us to believe you?'

Isabel stared back at me belligerently. 'Believe what you like. I admit to hitting Libby with that branch. I thought I'd killed her, but the stupid girl must have a thicker skull than I thought. As for Rick Browning, nobody knew who he was.' She glanced across at Julian, who was still looking shell-shocked. 'You tell them. Go on, man, show a bit of backbone.'

Julian cleared his throat before speaking. 'We only found out who he was when I unwrapped the bandages from his face after we'd found the body. As soon as I saw who it was, I knew we were in for big trouble. It's an open secret that relations between Browning and me were poor. I was afraid I'd be blamed.'

Isabel gave a scornful hiss. 'He was terrified. The brave soldier was close to tears, weren't you, darling?' There was nothing affectionate in the way she used the word. 'He grabbed my arm and scuttled off like a sheep running from a wolf.'

'And that's the last you saw of the body? The next time you went up there was after the police had finished their search and you went up with your bit of wood to draw your phoney tracks in the earth?'

Julian nodded but I saw Isabel shake her head. 'It's the last time Mr Courageous here saw the body but it was my idea to turn it to the company's advantage, so I went up there when it started to get dark with some petrol and set the body on fire.' She glared at Julian, who was looking quite overcome. 'I told *you* to do it and you were too scared, weren't you? Just too damn scared.' I waited for her to spit at him, but she restrained herself.

Fournier and I exchanged glances. That appeared to explain the fire, but we were still a long way from discovering who had been responsible for Brown's death – assuming these two weren't lying. I felt pretty sure that she, at least, was telling the truth, not just about this but about everything now. I'd seen it happen numerous times in my career. When a certain kind of perpetrator finally realises that there's no escape, the barriers come down and they come out with pure, unadulterated truth. I decided to try and capitalise on this.

'You said you heard a scream, followed by running footsteps. Did you see the person running away?' Both of them shook their heads so I tried again. 'What about on your way up the track before you got to the crime scene? Did you pass anybody on the way?'

Isabel shook her head but this time Julian spoke up. 'Yes, I did. I stopped in the trees for a pee as we were walking up and I got the fright of my life. There in the shadows, I found myself face to face with Wayne, lurking behind a tree. I assumed he'd gone in there for the same reason I had. I felt embarrassed and he looked the same. No words were exchanged and I got out of there as soon as possible.'

I shook my head in disbelief. 'And when we were questioning you on Wednesday, you didn't think it worth mentioning?'

'To be quite honest, after the awful shock I had only a few minutes later, I had completely forgotten about it until now. I was pretty sure he was just there having a pee the same as I was. Surely it doesn't mean he killed Browning, does it?'

Pierre listened to my translation and then replied in sombre tones. 'That's what we need to find out.'

23

SATURDAY AFTERNOON

After Isabel had been loaded into a waiting patrol car and taken off to Aosta, Pierre left to drive back to Cervinia for his appointment at the *Carabinieri* barracks and I went across to the group by the fire to give them the news.

'I'm now in a position to tell you that the attack on Libby, although vicious and life-threatening, didn't kill her after all. She's been in a coma since the attack but she's just woken up and has revealed that her assailant was Isabel. In consequence, Isabel has been arrested. I'm sorry we had to maintain the fiction she'd been killed, but it was in order to help us find the culprit.'

I kept my eyes on the ufologists. They were all there – apart from Julian, who had disappeared back to his motorhome in considerable distress – and, as far as I could see, the reaction of all of them was the same. Val summed it up perfectly.

'How absolutely wonderful, and we thought she was dead! That poor girl, and that awful, evil woman. Isabel deserves everything that's coming to her.'

'Will Libby be all right?' Sandra was looking mightily relieved, but presumably she hadn't yet worked out that although we had caught one would-be killer, there was still Brown's murder to be solved. For now, I didn't disabuse her.

'We hope so. The fact that she's awake and rational is a very positive sign, so fingers crossed.'

Wayne was looking positively euphoric at the news, but that didn't last long. I exchanged glances with Fournier and then asked Wayne to accompany us to the tent for further questioning. As we left the campfire, I caught Alice's eye and she gave me a quizzical look but, for now, I gave no response. We still had to get Wayne's side of the story.

As soon as we had sat down, I put the question to him. 'We understand from Julian that around six o'clock on Tuesday, you were hiding in the bushes in the vicinity of Rick Brown's murder. Can you confirm that and can you tell us why you didn't mention it before?'

He fidgeted nervously and took off his hat to run his hand across his forehead, which was damp with sweat. Outside, it was still warm in spite of the absence of direct sunshine, but I had little doubt that this perspiration had a different origin. 'Like I told you before, I was out on Tuesday afternoon and evening taking background footage for the programme we're making about the UFO phenomena around the Matterhorn.'

'So if you were just out taking pictures, why did Julian find you hiding in the bushes?'

'I just went into the woods for a pee.'

He was staring down at his hands and I could see his fingers twisting and turning nervously. I had no doubt at all that there was more to this story than just a comfort break, so I leant on him a bit more.

'The fact is, Wayne, that although Julian and Isabel were going *up* the track, you were quite obviously coming *down* the track and only a hundred metres or so further up was where a murder took place. Think very carefully before you answer my next question: did you kill Richard Brown?'

He raised his eyes and stared straight at me. 'No, I didn't. I've never killed anybody and I would never kill anybody.'

From what Julian and Isabel had said – assuming they were telling the truth – it was clear that Wayne couldn't be the murderer because they claimed to have heard the scream and the running feet several minutes later, by which time Wayne would have been some distance away, possibly already back at the camp, but I needed to keep him under pressure until he told us the truth about what he knew.

'We know that your history with Richard Brown was troubled and violent. You've already admitted that you assaulted him at your previous place of work and I put it to you that you recognised him when he arrived here on Monday, and on Tuesday evening, you followed him into the woods and killed him.' I subjected him to my fiercest stare. 'You did, didn't you?'

'No, no, no, I didn't kill him...' His voice tailed off but I said nothing, preferring to let him stew. A full minute passed before he looked up again and, this time, I read fear in his eyes. 'I didn't follow him into the woods; I met him coming up the track as I was coming back to the camp, but you're completely wrong if you think I killed him.'

'And did you recognise him?'

He nodded.

'When did you recognise him? As soon as he arrived on Monday? Later on? At the moment when you ran into him in the woods? When?'

'Tuesday after lunch. He was sitting opposite me by the camp-fire and it suddenly came to me. Underneath those bandages, I felt sure I knew him. When you've held somebody by the throat and stared into his eyes at close range like I have, you remember them.'

'And did you say anything to him or to any of the others? To Julian, maybe?'

'No, I didn't say anything to anybody.' There was a more defiant look in his eyes. 'It wasn't anybody's business but mine.'

'What sort of business? Unfinished business?'

He fell silent again but I just sat there and waited. Finally, he nodded slowly. 'Listen, I didn't tell you the whole truth before. I didn't leave CosmosLink by choice, I was sacked, and I was sacked because Rick told the producer I had assaulted him and he refused to work with me. He told a whole lot of lies about me supposedly propositioning one of his girlfriends. They were lies, horrible lies.' His voice was rising in volume and intensity. 'When I told you I only shook him by the throat, I was telling the truth, but if they hadn't dragged me off him, I would have punched his lights out.'

'Let's get this straight, Wayne. You're telling me that you recognised him on Tuesday afternoon and then quite by chance, you ran into him in the woods later on, but you didn't kill him. What happened when you saw him? Did you confront him? Presumably, he'd already recognised you.'

'Yes, he'd recognised me all right.' His voice returned to normal pitch. 'He just stood there on the track, cocky as you like, and I knew he was smirking underneath those bandages. He said, "You always were a bit slow, Wayne. It's taken you long enough to realise who I am." And he just stood there, blocking my way.'

'And then what happened?'

'I put down the camera and I punched him.'

'What, there, in the middle of the track?'

'Yes, and I heard his nose crack.' He looked up again and his eyes were now unnaturally bright as he relived the moment of his revenge. 'And it felt good, really good.'

'And what happened then?'

'Do you know what he did? He burst into tears like a little girl and then he turned tail and ran.'

'He ran where?'

'Up the hill into the trees, away from the track. There are all sorts of paths there. He was terrified I'd hit him again, but I didn't need to.' There was satisfaction in his voice now. 'I just stood there and listened to him crashing through the undergrowth as he ran further and further away, and then there was silence. He must have stopped.'

'And what did you do then?'

'Nothing.'

'Nothing?'

'I just picked up the camera and went back to the camp for a mug of Val's tea.' He stopped and corrected himself. 'Although, when I heard somebody coming up the track, I nipped into the bushes to hide. I didn't expect Julian to come in after me so I just bluffed it out, pretending I wanted a pee.'

'And did you see anybody else out there on the track, either coming or going?'

'Apart from Julian, no, nobody.'

I got him to repeat his story twice more and pressed him for more information each time but he remained steadfast. Finally, I sent him out of the tent and looked across at Fournier.

'True? False? A bit of both? What do you think?'

'I think he was telling the truth. After all, the pathologist said the victim had a broken nose and none of the suspects here could have known that. I believe he punched him, but I don't necessarily think he killed him.'

I nodded. 'I tend to agree. Yes, it's possible he first broke Brown's nose and then pursued him uphill through the trees until he caught up with him and killed him with the big rock, but, like you, I tend to believe the man. Also, I've been wondering what

Brown was doing fifty yards off the beaten track and that explains it: he was running away from Wayne. Which leaves us with the question of: if Wayne isn't our killer, then who is? I'm still convinced it's one of the group. As far as we know, the only other person who knew his true identity beneath the bandages was Alice Turner, but she claims to have been down at Montaz, and there's CCTV evidence that she was at the hotel that evening. Of course, it's possible that she found some way of sneaking back to kill Brown or, quite possibly, that she told one of the other ufologists about him. Alternatively, maybe one of the others recognised him, just like Wayne O'Connell did. But we need a motive.'

'As far as I can see, the only person with a motive is Julian Goodfellow. He despised Brown and would have taken a very dim view of having a spy in the camp, but murder...?'

'When we interviewed Julian and Isabel the other day, I definitely got the impression that Isabel knew Brown well. Certainly, she looked quite overwhelmed to find out he was the mystery man who'd been killed. What if she was having an affair with Brown, and Julian found out? That would give him even more reason to commit murder. You've got the passports, haven't you? Could I have a look at them?'

'They're in the car. Give me a minute.'

Fournier was back almost immediately and I took the passports eagerly. 'Let's try something.'

I picked out the passports belonging to Isabel, Julian and Rick Brown. All three passports contained numerous pages stamped with entry and exit visas for countries as varied as Chile, India and even Iceland. I gave Brown's to Fournier and asked him to make a list of places visited with arrival and departure dates, while I did the same for Julian's passport and then moved onto Isabel's. It took us almost twenty minutes but we finally had three lists and we worked our way through them, putting them into chronological order. Most of Isabel's trips coincided with Julian's, which made sense as they would have been travelling and working together. A few of Brown's also mirrored them – presumably the occasions on which, as Julian had said, Brown had been following them while they were on research trips. There were a couple of trips that the individual passport holders had clearly undertaken alone, but there were no fewer than four occasions over the past twelve months when Isabel and Rick Brown had both been in the same places on the same days – and nights – but without Julian.

When we finally got to the end of the list, Fournier beamed at me and banged his fist on the table. 'That's it, we've got him. Isabel and Brown were having an affair. Julian Goodfellow discovered this and a mixture of jealousy as well as professional dislike was enough for him to murder Brown on Tuesday night. Well done, Dan!'

I sat back but, instead of sharing his jubilation, I had a feeling of anti-climax. It certainly looked as though we had enough evidence now to proceed with a murder charge against Julian, but somewhere at the back of my old copper's brain, I harboured a nagging doubt. When we had spoken to him earlier and he had forcefully denied any involvement in Brown's murder, the fact was that I had believed him and, in spite of this new evidence, I still did. Although I could tell that Fournier was chomping at the bit, dying to go across to Julian's van and arrest him, I urged caution – for now at least.

'Julian can't go anywhere at the moment. If I were you, I'd leave the roadblock at the bottom of the track just in case. Why don't you go back to the station in Aosta and confront Isabel with what we've just worked out? Your English is good enough for that; I've heard you. As far as I can see, she has nothing to lose by telling us the truth about her relations with Brown. From her attitude earlier, I don't think there's any question of her being prepared to lie to protect Julian if he's guilty – in fact, the way she was treating him, she'd probably jump at the chance to bring him down along with her. Ask her to confirm whether Julian might have been able to slip away before the two of them set off up the hill to the observation post. She said they were together when they found the body but maybe he might have had a window of opportunity to go and kill Brown first. Can you do that?'

'Yes, of course, but...' I could tell he was dying to arrest Julian ASAP.

I carried on. 'It looks very likely that Isabel and Brown were having an affair so try to pin her down on exactly when Julian found out about the two of them. If she confirms that Julian knew about the affair before the murder and also that he recognised Brown when the man turned up swathed in bandages, then I think we'll have a strong case. I'd prefer to get confirmation from her before we arrest Julian. Are you happy with that?'

He patently wasn't, and I could tell that all his instincts were urging him to clap a pair of handcuffs on Julian and cart him off to the station immediately but, good man that he was, Fournier just nodded and agreed to do as I had asked.

After he had left, I sat in the tent for some time, thinking back on the afternoon's events and the new facts now in our possession, doing my best to think of any possible motive any of the remaining suspects might have had to kill Brown. I was just about to get up and go for a walk with Oscar when a thought occurred to me. I had a feeling in my bones that the suicide of Brown's former lady friend, Tracey Burgess, might still have a connection somehow or other and it occurred to me to ask a question I hadn't asked Jess when she told me about it. I decided it would be quicker to go through Scotland Yard rather than bother her again so I called Paul.

I gave him this afternoon's news and confirmed that Isabel had been arrested for the attempted murder of Libby and then I asked a favour. 'Could you just check something for me, please? At the end of January this year, a woman called Tracey Burgess killed herself in Brixton. Could you just check if she either was, or had been, married and, if so, what her maiden name was? That would be a big help.'

At the end of the call, I looked down at the Labrador snoozing at my feet.

'How about a walk, Oscar?'

He leapt to his feet with an expression on his face that told me that had been a rhetorical question.

24

SATURDAY LATE AFTERNOON

Oscar and I walked down through the forest to the convent. On the way, we played fetch and he plunged joyfully into the undergrowth to locate the sticks I threw for him. Up above us, the sky was now completely overcast. From time to time, the trees thinned and spectacular views out over the high Alps opened up before me, their peaks now concealed in the growing cloud. I breathed deeply, relishing the aroma of resin, bark and moss, and reflected on how it could be that such an idyllic place had sparked such vicious assaults. I spared a thought for Libby, who would no doubt have a long road to recovery ahead, and I hoped everything would go well for Carmela and her baby. I pulled out my phone and called Anna, more to hear her voice than for anything else, and I told her about the latest developments. We knew each other so well by now, and she must have picked up something in my voice.

'You sound a bit down. What's the matter? Haven't you just solved one case and it sounds as if you're close to solving the other? Surely you should be happy.'

'I hope we solve it, I really hope so.' At that moment, Oscar must have spotted a squirrel as he charged off into the trees, barking furiously. The squirrel probably wouldn't have agreed with me, but I found it a charming scene and the sound of the barking echoing through the trees and around the valley made such a pleasant change from the sounds of the big city that I found myself smiling. 'I'm fine, Anna. Just feeling my age, I expect. I must admit that in my final years at the Met, it started getting to me on occasions. The stupidity of some people and the plain evil they commit can get a bit wearing, but it's all right, I've got you and I've got Oscar, but I wish you could be here to see these wonderful mountains with me. It's too beautiful here for anybody to feel depressed for too long.'

'Well, I wish I were there with you, too. Come home soon, *carissimo*. Oh, by the way, I have a message for you from Zia Menca. She said to tell you, "The fact that you can't see something doesn't mean that it isn't there." Any idea what she means?'

'No idea at all – I imagine she's talking about little green men. Anyway, do thank her from me. *Ciao*.'

Down at the convent, I found Conrad and he had news, not about the investigation but about himself.

'Good afternoon, sir. You can be one of the first people to know – I've finally got all my papers in order. I can legally live and work in Italy and I've been offered a job.' He was beaming from ear to ear. I was delighted for him and I clapped him on the back.

'Conrad, after the past few days, I needed some good news and I'm so happy for you. We have to celebrate. Do you think Don Piero would mind if I bought us both a drink?'

At that moment, the old priest himself emerged from the convent door and came over to where we were standing. Oscar wandered across to meet him and Don Piero ruffled his ears with one hand as he gave me a little wave with the other. 'Good afternoon, *Commissario*, is it true you've caught the killer?'

I had no idea why he had decided to award me the title, but I didn't bother to set him straight. Internally, I was marvelling at the almost magical way news travelled here in the mountains.

'Conrad's just told me his good news and I'd like to buy him a drink to celebrate. Would you like to join us, Don Piero?' To add a bit of syrup to the invitation, I added, 'I'll tell you how we're getting on with the investigation.'

He looked around and the only other customers were a young couple at a distant table clearly far more interested in each other. He returned his attention to the two of us and grinned. 'I have a bottle of very good spumante in the fridge, just waiting for a suitable moment of celebration. It's from a little place called Monforte, just outside Barolo, where I spent fifteen years as the parish priest. The parishioners still send me a dozen bottles each year and now is definitely the right moment to open one of them.' His grin broadened. 'Or two.'

He disappeared back into the convent and reappeared a minute later with a bottle and glasses, along with the two groundsmen I had seen working here the other day. We all sat down around a table and Don Piero filled the glasses and distributed them. He raised his glass towards Conrad and gave him a warm smile. 'A toast. To my new foreman, Conrad. I couldn't be happier that you've decided to stick around.'

We all drank to Conrad's new position and chatted about life here in the Alps and how different it must feel for people coming from so far afield. I confirmed that the police had apprehended the perpetrator who had so nearly cost a young woman her life. Don Piero nodded approvingly and asked about Brown's murderer, but all I could do for now was to assure him that we believed we were getting close.

Three quarters of an hour later, we got a whole lot closer. My phone rang and it was Paul with some very useful information. 'I've checked up on that suicide case. Tracey Burgess, age thirty-eight, died of an overdose on the thirtieth of January this year, only three months ago. Sounds like she had a tough life. You were right, she had been married to a William Burgess, but he also took his own life five years ago. She actually found his body in the garage of their house in Brixton. God knows what sort of effect that must have had on her. Anyway, her maiden name was Phillips. Does that help?'

'I think it does, thanks, Paul. I'll let you know how it goes, but now I need to make a call.'

As it turned out, I didn't need to make the call. No sooner had I finished speaking to Paul than my phone started ringing. It was Fournier and he sounded less excited than before. 'Isabel Sanchez says that she told Julian Goodfellow about her affair with Brown on Thursday afternoon, in the course of the quarrel they had when he told her he was giving her job to Elizabeth Winter. So if that's true, it means that Goodfellow didn't know about Brown and her before the murder, so it goes a long way towards clearing him, doesn't it? Also, she swears she and he were together before the murder so that's another reason he couldn't have done it. You were right to be cautious.'

'Don't worry about that, Fournier; there's something you need to do for me. I've just been told that the woman who killed herself in London after being dumped by Brown had previously been married, and her maiden name was Phillips. I'm pretty sure I remember seeing that name on one of the passports when we were going through them earlier. Please could you check that for me?'

'I've just come out of the custody unit and the passports are in my bag in the office. Give me ten minutes and I'll get back to you.'

The call came through as I was walking back up to the camp and it confirmed my hypothesis that the suicide of Tracey Burgess and the murder of Brown were indeed linked. I told him to get himself up to Montaz as soon as possible and then I got in the van and drove down to the hotel. When I got there, I saw Alice's car parked in its usual spot alongside the hotel and I found her in the bar, sitting alone at a table, writing on her laptop. She looked up as she saw me and smiled, pointing to the half-empty bottle of red on the table in front of her.

'Hi, Dan, grab a glass and come and join me.'

I walked over and sat down, not bothering with getting a glass. Across the table from her, I observed her reaction as I asked the question. 'Tell me about Tracey. She was your sister, wasn't she?'

The smile on her face was washed away in an instant. At first, she said nothing, just reached for the bottle to fill her glass to the rim, but after a full minute, she finally looked back up at me again, and I could see the tears sparkling in her eyes.

'I said you were a good detective, didn't I?' She pulled out a tissue and wiped her eyes before taking a couple of big mouthfuls of Dutch courage. 'Yes, Tracey was my little sister.'

'And she took her own life as a result of Brown's poor treatment of her?'

'She got pregnant, Dan, and when she told him, he just left her.' Her expression hardened into a bitter frown. 'Discarded her like a used rag. He was a horrible, horrible man. I had no choice.'

I felt my phone vibrate and saw that it was a text from Jess in London.

Spoke to a friend at the Mirror who told me they didn't send Alice Turner to Italy. She's been signed off for the past few months and receiving counselling for acute depression. Her articles about Brown just started arriving on the editor's desk early this week. Thought you might be interested. Jess. x

I set the phone down on the table and pressed the Voice Record button, determined to do this by the book. 'Listen, Alice, I know you've had a tough time – first your husband and then your sister, all within a few weeks of each other. I know you've been receiving treatment for depression and you're not a well woman.' I murmured a silent thank you to Jess for her perfectly timed text. 'Do you want to tell me about what happened on Tuesday evening?' I made sure I kept my expression and my voice as understanding and as gentle as I could. My four-legged friend must have picked up on this, as he gave up the assiduous search for crumbs he had been conducting beneath the table and went across to sit at Alice's side, resting his nose on her thigh. Consoled by his support, she took another mouthful of wine and started talking.

'I'd been trying to get him on his own for weeks. The trouble was that he did a lot of travelling overseas and it was hard to catch up with him. Then, quite by chance last week, a journalist friend who specialises in medical stories mentioned that he'd heard Brown was going to Switzerland to have some cosmetic work done on his face. I followed him to Montreux and from there, like I already told you, it was easy for me to tail him up to here.'

'Did he know who you were? Had you ever met him when he was with your sister?'

She shook her head. 'I never had the pleasure.' She made a sour face, took another mouthful of wine, and then carried on before I needed to prompt her. 'On Tuesday, it was quite easy. I parked my car at the side of the hotel, not the front, so the CCTV couldn't pick it up. I knew that he was going up to his shift at the observation post starting at six, so at a quarter past five, I slipped out into the garden through my French windows. That way, I avoided the CCTV in reception.' She caught my eye and even managed a hint of a smile. 'Like I told you, I'm an investigative journalist. I notice stuff like that. I drove up to a place I'd earmarked, just a short way before the police roadblock, where I could hide the car. Ironically, it was only a hundred yards from where poor Libby's car ended up two days later. I made my way uphill through the trees and lay in wait near the track, hoping Brown would be on his own.'

'And was he?'

'It all got a bit weird. There I was, crouching in the bushes near the track, expecting to see him come up that way, but then the next thing I heard was crashing footsteps as somebody came running up through the trees *behind* me. I stayed dead still and he didn't see me. As he went past, I recognised that it was Brown. Nobody seemed to be following him and nobody was with him, so I got to my feet and hurried up the hill after him. I found him on his hands and knees, panting like a dog, completely out of breath. As I stared down at him all my bottled-up emotion overflowed and I knew what I had to do.'

She broke off for another mouthful of wine, after which she emptied the remains of the bottle into her glass before picking up her story again. 'There was a big lump of rock lying close by. I picked it up and went across to him, but he was so occupied with trying to staunch a bloody nose that he only looked up and saw me at the last moment. I lifted the rock above my head and smashed it down onto him. Just before I did it, I looked him square in the eye and said, "This is for Tracey." I knew as soon as the rock hit him that he was dead. I just hope his last thoughts were of what a bastard he'd been to my sister.' She raised her eyes to the heavens and blew a little kiss. 'I did it for you, Trace, I did it for you.' Tears ran slowly down her cheeks.

Her story told, she sat back and drank more wine while I absorbed what she had just told me. It all fitted with what Wayne had said and it was now clear that Isabel's story of coming back later to set fire to the body must also be correct.

We had our murderer, but I felt little sense of achievement. A bad man had been killed by a sick woman. All I felt was deep sympathy for Alice and for her sister. My years on the force told me there was never an excuse for killing another human being but both women had had some tough breaks. As ever acutely aware of the mood of the room, Oscar rose up on his hind legs and put his front paws on Alice's lap, stretching up to lick the tears that continued to roll down her cheeks. In the distance, I could hear an approaching siren as Fournier had broken all speed limits to get back to the hotel.

We had solved the murder at the Matterhorn but, for once in my career, I almost wished we hadn't.

25

SATURDAY NIGHT

I had dinner on my own at the hotel – one last *bistecca alla valdostana* as I would be setting off back to Florence next day – and I spent most of the meal deep in thought. My spirits were lifted at just before nine by a phone call from Aosta. To my surprise, it was Inspector Carmela Costey.

'*Ciao*, Dan, I've just heard the news. Congratulations.'

'Thanks, but it was very much a team effort. You did most of the work before you went off and Fournier was great. My friends in the UK provided the snippets of information that made it possible to pull all the threads together. So, like I say, teamwork. How about you? How are you?'

'I'm fine, thanks, just a bit tired and David's fine as well.'

'Your husband?'

'My son. David was born just over an hour ago.'

I was stunned for a moment and then I found myself laughing in disbelief. 'You gave birth to your son and an hour later, you're already thinking about police matters? Inspector Costey, you're bonkers. Haven't you got better things to do – like sleeping for a week, for example?'

I heard her laugh in return. 'Chance would be a fine thing. There's nothing wrong with little David's lungs and I think he's inherited his father's appetite. Anyway, look, I just wanted to say a huge thank you, and if there's ever anything I can do for you, just say the word.'

At the end of the meal, I roused myself to take Oscar for his evening walk and on impulse, I loaded him into the van and we drove up to the camp for the last time. The police roadblock had disappeared and I found all the ufologists sitting around the camp-fire, needless to say, most of them drinking tea – although Wilfred was hugging his grappa bottle. Even Julian had abandoned his campervan and he was sitting there as well. I went across to greet them.

'Have you heard the news?' I was fully expecting to be the bearer of the news that the murderer had been apprehended, but it transpired that the Montaz bush telegraph worked both ways. While I had been eating my dinner, word about Alice's arrest had mysteriously spread all the way up here.

Val answered for all of them. 'We're just so relieved that it's over. Would you like a cuppa?'

I had just had an espresso but I felt it rude to say no, so I sat down with them and sipped a steaming hot mug of tea while answering the questions they all started throwing at me. When I got up to take Oscar for his walk, I queried who was manning the observation post and was disappointed by the response from Julian of all people.

'None of us felt like going up there tonight. Last night, there were no lights and nothing today either. I'm afraid we've fright-ened them off. Besides, the cloud cover means we'd see very little anyway and I'm not in the mood.'

He sounded so depressed, I knew I had to do my best to snap them out of it. I swallowed the last of my tea and stood up. 'Well, I for one am going up there. This is my last night here and I want to see something worthwhile. Come on, who's with me?'

Sandra and Maggie immediately jumped to their feet and gradually, they were followed by the others until only Julian was left sitting there. I walked across to him and tapped him on the shoulder.

'Come on, Julian, you're the leader, so lead!'

He looked up at me. 'After everything that's happened, my heart's not in it.' But I could tell he was wavering. Val grabbed one of his arms and Sybil the other and they frogmarched him up the track while we all followed.

When we got up to the observation post, it looked quite spooky. Only a few hundred metres above our heads was the base of the thick covering of cloud that had been building throughout the day. What little light there was reflected against the underside of the cloud, making it look as if we were in a huge cavern. It felt quite oppressive and I rather regretted suggesting we should come up here, but we were here now so I settled down on the ground with my back against a boulder and stared out across the valley. I could make out little clusters of lights below us and over on the opposite hillside, but the mountains themselves had been swallowed up by the cloud. I heard a voice at my ear. It was Val, for once not offering a cuppa.

'Will Libby be all right?'

I looked up at her and found that my eyes had now so successfully adapted to the dark that I could make out her facial features even without moon or starlight. 'I believe so. The sergeant told me this evening that he's heard that the medics say she's making amazing progress.'

'That's good. And what about Alice? Will she go to jail for a long time?'

I'd been thinking about this. 'I doubt it. She was already

receiving medical care for her mental health and I'm sure any judge would take that into account. Maybe she was on medication as well, who knows? I imagine she will have to go to prison, or more probably a secure unit, for a while, but if she gets the right treatment, I see no reason why she shouldn't emerge from this whole business able to pick up her life again.'

'I do hope so.'

The hum of conversation died down and I settled back against my rock with Oscar sprawled at my feet. After all the excitement of the day – and far too much food and drink – I felt my eyelids grow heavy but as I was almost drifting off, the weirdest thing happened.

There was no noise whatsoever, no sign of anything in the sky, but for some strange reason, I found my eyes drawn to the right, in the direction of the Matterhorn, which was, by now, swathed in cloud. I found myself involuntarily tracking something in the sky that I couldn't see, but which I somehow knew to be coming down the valley through the clouds towards me. I felt my head slowly turn as the invisible object came past until I was looking straight ahead of me into blackness. As I did so, I distinctly felt a pulse of energy pass through me and the hair on the back of my neck and my forearms stood up on end. Whatever it was, I wasn't the only one to feel this invisible presence. Oscar roused himself from his sleep and stood up, his nose pointing in the exact same direction as my eyes, and his tail began to wag in friendly greeting.

I glanced down at my watch. It was three minutes to midnight but, bizarrely, the second hand had stopped moving. I felt a presence all around me, which should have been scary but the sight of my dog wagging his tail at this invisible visitor kept me from freaking out. I just sat there and stared and stared and stared... at nothing.

I was roused from my daze by a touch on the shoulder and the sound of Val's voice.

'Wake up, Dan, it's gone one o'clock and it's starting to rain. You'll get wet.'

I blinked a few times and turned towards her. I must have looked completely out of it because a note of concern entered her voice. 'Are you all right, Dan? You look as if you've seen a ghost.'

'Did you feel it?' I was finding it remarkably difficult to get my words out.

'Feel what?'

'A presence, something invisible.' I ran my hand over my forehead, registering that it came away damp as the drizzle intensified. 'Maybe I was dreaming.'

'You looked as if you were miles away. Come on now, we need to get back to camp before the mist descends on us and we can't see a thing.'

As I pulled myself to my feet, I was reminded of Zia Menca's cryptic message: *The fact that you can't see something doesn't mean that it isn't there.* I checked my watch and turned to Val.

'What did you say the time was?'

Julian answered. 'It's just past one o'clock.'

The second hand on my watch was moving again, but the time showing was two minutes to midnight. I had lost an hour of my life. I looked down at Oscar, who was standing in front of me, his tail wagging slowly.

'What the hell's going on, Oscar?'

His tail began to wag harder.

He knew the truth.

ACKNOWLEDGMENTS

To my lovely editor, Emily Ruston, and all the team at my exceptional publishers, Boldwood Books. Special thanks to Sue Smith and Emily Reader for pointing out my errors and keeping me on the straight and narrow. Warm thanks as always to Simon Mattacks for his excellent narration that brings the characters to life. Thanks also to my big brother for helping me decide how to kill people (!). Thanks to my old friend, Tony Stevenson, for his classical expertise and finally, thanks to my ever-patient wife, Mariangela, for all the times she has read and commented on the book as it developed.

ABOUT THE AUTHOR

T. A. Williams is the author of over twenty bestselling romances for HQ and Canelo and is now turning his hand to cosy crime, set in his beloved Italy, for Boldwood. The series introduces us to DCI Armstrong and his labrador Oscar. Trevor lives in Devon with his Italian wife.

Sign up to T. A. Williams' mailing list here for news, competitions and updates on future books.

Visit T. A. Williams' website: http://www.tawilliamsbooks.com

Follow T. A. Williams' on social media:

x.com/TAWilliamsBooks

facebook.com/TrevorWilliamsBooks

ALSO BY T. A. WILLIAMS

The Armstrong and Oscar Cozy Mystery Series

Murder in Tuscany

Murder in Chianti

Murder in Florence

Murder in Siena

Murder at the Matterhorn

Poison
& Pens

POISON & PENS IS THE HOME OF
COZY MYSTERIES SO POUR YOURSELF
A CUP OF TEA & GET SLEUTHING!

DISCOVER PAGE-TURNING NOVELS FROM
YOUR FAVOURITE AUTHORS &
MEET NEW FRIENDS

JOIN OUR
FACEBOOK GROUP

BIT.LYPOISONANDPENSFB

SIGN UP TO OUR
NEWSLETTER

BIT.LY/POISONANDPENSNEWS

Boldwood

Boldwood Books is an award-winning fiction publishing company seeking out the best stories from around the world.

Find out more at www.boldwoodbooks.com

Join our reader community for brilliant books, competitions and offers!

Follow us
@BoldwoodBooks
@TheBoldBookClub

Sign up to our weekly deals newsletter

https://bit.ly/BoldwoodBNewsletter

Made in the USA
Columbia, SC
28 September 2024

43188492R00128